The Protectors
Preface

The time is in the future, and the world has changed. This story is about a young boy, Josh, and his AL-LI (Artificial Living Linguistic Intelligence) robot named Noah. Josh, a pre-teen boy in a home of a non-present, alcoholic father, navigates through life with ease since the innovation of AL-LI robots being made available in every home. Josh has even learned hacks in the program of AL-LI that has Noah helping him with homework and helps him to engage in a pre-teen world of curiosity and gameplay with his friends Yashi, Terra, and Bub.

The company that invented AL-LI is called ProTech, and its founder, Dek Bale, have found that convenience and influence are worth the investment in government bureaucrats to look the other way in the ethical and political legislation regarding the amount of control of AL-LIs in the country. Bale is in line to gain even more control, power, and wealth as he has presented to the United States about AL-LIs becoming the military. Bale is willing to do whatever it takes to protect his contract.

Josh believes though that Noah is different, and with his friends, they set out on a path to prove otherwise with the adventure of a lifetime that takes them down a deep, dark path of what people are willing to accept and depend upon for their own personal convenience and the understanding of where true protection originates.

Contents

Part 1: Power On

Introduction: An Artificial Reality	1
Chapter 1: Life in Valley Hills for Josh	6
Chapter 2: Life with Noah	10
Chapter 3: When Everything Changed	18
Chapter 4: A Reset Begins	27
Chapter 5: Home Security	36
Chapter 6: Finding Help	50
Chapter 7: A Link is Found	56
Chapter 8: Hacking the Firewall	67
Chapter 9: The Crash	82
Chapter 10: The Miracle	91

Part 2: Restart   96

Chapter 11: Breakthrough	99
Chapter 12: System Preferences	106
Chapter 13: Search Engine	115
Chapter 14: The Code	123
Chapter 15: Decoding	133
Chapter 16: Following	141
Chapter 17: Contact Tracing	152
Chapter 18: Profile Update	163
Chapter 19: The Escape Button	171
Chapter 20: Unfinished	188

Part 3: Shutdown	192
Chapter 21: Search History	195
Chapter 22: Key Code	205
Chapter 23: Generations	211
Chapter 24: Viral	216
Chapter 25: Incognito Mode	224
Chapter 26: Friends List	235
Chapter 27: Mother's Board	242
Conclusion: Restored	262

Part 1. Power On

Introduction: An Artificial Reality

"Welcome to Valley Hills; A City of ProTech" reads the sign as you enter the city. Valley Hills is not a city with a past; in fact, the city has only been in existence for eleven years, since the founding of ProTech, a technology company. When the state of California divided in the early 21st century into three states (North California, South California, and East California), North California desired to create new cities that embraced technology and were built around its use in the city. The state of North California welcomed innovations to be experimented and employed in the home. Protech emerged as one of the pioneers in the industry, to the point of creating their city.

Valley Hills has the look of being a quaint city with landscaped sidewalks and seemingly perfect exteriors of every home that you pass. Amid the beauty is the persistent use of technology. All the fast-food restaurants are operated by computer engineers, using AI technology.

In an effort for the city to remain environment-friendly- there is the use of electric rail systems and individual tubes that transport people throughout the city. In schools, students engage in pure technological innovations that are designed to tailor the learning experience to the child's specific needs.

The education system of Valley Hills is unique in its philosophy. There is a lesser emphasis placed upon general education, and the focus is placed on the needs of ProTech's industry. Topics such as coding, computer engineering, and application development are taught at an early age. The science fair each year in the school is viewed as one of the highlight events as students are able to show off to ProTech engineers their best innovative ideas.

Valley Hills is not without its share of issues as well. Due to the enclosed nature of the city and consistent push from ProTech for innovation, the need to decompress from the stresses of work has brought about entertainment and de-stress culture. Any entertainment need is presented, and opportunities to experience indulgences are encouraged. Therefore, many marriages struggle with the demands placed on the husbands and wives that work for ProTech. Therefore, having a family in Valley Hills is hard and can present many issues with how to care for children the best.

The introduction of artificial intelligence in the home in the 2010s brought about an extreme revolution of robots introduced into the home life. Initially, the push was for Roomba's and Echo's. Still, now with the founding of ProTech, the introduction of life-sized technology has become a commonplace in the United States home.

ProTech's patented Artificial Living Linguistic Intelligence (Al-LI, pronounced ally) technology allowed not only for the robots to have human-like features of a face and skin, but they are also able to respond to situations, be funny, and interact in human situations. One of the unique features of AL-LI is their learning and anticipation technology that has brought about the ability for the AL-LIs to demonstrate interactive capabilities far beyond their predecessors. This technology was developed by Dek Bale, the founder of Pro-Tech. The idea that Bale presented in his capabilities spoke directly to the family dynamic. It was there that the AL-LI took on the role of being a servant, teacher, babysitter, confidante, and in some rare cases, friend.

The outside world is looking in as ethical and political lines of legislation for AL-LIs have become blurred. The economic ripples have been challenged regarding their regulation and interaction within human society. As people have become accustomed to the convenience provided by their AL-LIs, they have often overlooked any ethical issues that arise. In a shocking move, ProTech provided an AL-LI as an advisor to the President to be able to provide information based upon world circumstances at a moment's notice.

Valley Hills had a limited police force as the city was covered in cameras, some that people never realized were not there. The only places that cameras were not allowed were in homes and areas on privacy. Often the police responded to actions that they saw on the cameras with their rolling patrols.

ProTech's security, however, seemingly operated under a different set of rules and always held a stronger influence over judicial matters than the Valley Hills police force. The security of ProTech also could override the AL-LI system that made NOAH's turn into additional security as needed.

At the center of Valley Hills was the campus of ProTech. The campus of ProTech was beaming with innovations and technology. From retinal scanners that are used for people to enter doors, to facial recognition at ProTech's cafeteria that began to prepare custom meals. At the center of the campus was a huge glass tower that had Dek Bale's house and office at the very top. From all parts of Valley Hill, the tower could be seen, even at night, when the tower would be in various colors based upon the closest holiday season.

Bale was a unique man with a small mustache and triangle beard. He always seemed to wear a jacket that had a variation of the color purple in the design with an onyx cane that he held close to him. He also wore large black square-rimmed glasses and had black hair with the part down the middle. He also loved the 90's hip-hop music, which was evident by his gold chain with a 24-karat golden boom box that hung in the middle.

Bale grew up in the technology boom in the late 1990s. He was considered a technology genius by age 12 and graduated from MIT at age 15. He was writing complex codes for various companies by age 17 and was one of the most sought-after code writers in the world. By age 21, he was named Time's Person of the Year. Slowly, his hand began to touch various technology projects, until he sought to start his own company, ProTech, at age 23.

Initially, Protech focused on security IT services for companies. Then, with a moment of innovation, Bale sought to expand into artificial intelligence for the home as the trends continued. Yet, ProTech struggled to define itself in an already bustling market niche.

Bale was rarely seen at ProTech or in public in general. His living quarters and office were heavily guarded, and a helicopter pad meant that Bale could leave whenever he wanted. Even when he had events to promote the next big innovative technology for ProTech, he would rarely make an appearance except to demonstrate the technology and then return to his glass tower.

Chapter 1

Life in Valley Hills for Josh

The life that Josh Nunley has known as a twelve-year-old boy has been Valley Hills and ProTech. His father, Cal Nunley, was one of the original key developers of the technology for ProTech as he worked with Bale. The demands that Bale placed upon Cal meant that he often felt obligated to stay engaged in his work, even while at home. For a young boy growing up around innovative technology, Josh was able to see projects and ideas that his father was working on. Still, other times it meant that he brought home the stress related to his work.
Josh never knew his mother, Deborah, that was a co-developer with Cal. While she was pregnant, she suffered a car wreck and died; however, the doctors were able to save Josh. Deborah's death devastated Cal to the point where there was a room called the "No-Go" in the house, where Cal had placed pictures and memorabilia of his life with Deborah all throughout the room. There were times when

Josh would sneak into the room, just to see the pictures of his mother and to try and understand who she was in her life. He was drawn to a particular picture of his mother that had her wearing a special necklace in the shape of a cross with a heart in the middle, and there was always a rose sitting in a vase beside the picture.

The memory of Deborah made it hard to celebrate Josh's birthday as it was greeted with bittersweet anticipation. Unfortunately, the way that Cal escaped the pain in his life was through his work. His work binges often ended with Cal yelling at Josh and breaking things throughout the house.

Cal realized early in Josh's life that he was in need of care so that his work for ProTech could not be impeded. Rather than hiring a babysitter, Cal brought home one of ProTech's newest prototypes, Noah. Noah (Nanny Overseer at Home) was the first human-like prototype from ProTech that was to serve as an AL-LI for the home. Similar to prior artificial intelligence systems, Noah could learn the skills and traits that were enabled with an app at a moment's notice. Due to Cal's absence and with the presence of technology, Josh became self-taught on the technology for Noah. He developed personal apps and skills for Noah that allowed him to become, at times, a personal playmate more than a nanny.

Some of the other unique features for Noah involved how his eyes served as cameras that Cal used to check in on Josh. There was even a mode that Cal could take over the voice of Noah and speak directly to Josh. Cal found himself watching Josh throughout the days, which drove him further into the dichotomy of work and being a father at home.

Cal, out of respect for Deborah's background, sought to expose Josh to spiritual matters by sending him to Valley Hills Church. It was the only church in Valley Hills, and it was required that no one religion was approved over another, which that anyone could attend, and the stories mixed different religious views. Even with this practice, attendees were few in number, and the preachers often spoke about a higher power that promoted positive thinking and how to not be stressful at work.

There were some groups of people that tried to meet in secret since they didn't agree with how ProTech monitored the churches; however, AL-LIs were programmed to report these findings to ProTech, and this led to people being fired or "conveniently removed" as it was referred. At an early age for Josh while in church, Noah often sat with him in the children's circle, with the teachers often looking and teaching Noah.

ProTech developed a program within the Noah that when they were in these teaching settings, the teachers could state the phrase "data input," and the AL-LIs would recognize this as new information and would listen to the discussion. Josh, when the teachers shared the Bible story about Noah and the flood, had the idea to start a catchphrase and hand motion when saying goodbye, "Two of everything," and they would each hold up the number two with their fingers and touch them together.

The difference with Noah lied in the innovative technology that ProTech developed and held close to the secret of their success. Cal worked specifically on the software that helped to develop the anticipation of pain for Noah. This innovation generally meant that

Cal worked on a certain line of code and app. Then Bale would personally apply his line of code that made it applicable to the AL-LI. Other skills for Noah included the judgment of human behavior, the ability to anticipate humor, and the ability to interact socially with humans.

Soon variations of Noah became common in Valley Hills and were doing everything from driving, cooking, writing, and singing. The world was on the outside looking into Valley Hills, seeking to understand what life could be like with the introduction of Noah's technology on the global stage.

Chapter 2

Life with Noah

The alarm clock for Josh began to ring with his favorite song and then soon the words began to ring out from the clock, "It's Friday, it's time to get ready for school, you have your test today in Mrs. Rogers class, I know you will have a great day." Then, as a means of motivation, Josh's TV in his room began to play a movie montage of famous climactic speeches, some humorous and some serious. Josh rolled over slowly and unwillingly and mumbled, "Can't I have five more minutes?" As he tried to close his eyes, the roar of an annoying pop song began to blast in his room.
He rolled over and grabbed the closest pillow to try and cover his ears. Realizing that the battle was to be a lost cause, he got up and said, "Ok, ok, I am up." The music died down, and a voice from his clock stated, "Excellent, Noah has breakfast ready for you downstairs."

Every morning, Josh woke up to the smell of bacon as Noah had fixed a hearty breakfast. There were times when Josh tried to resist eating, and Noah could patch immediately to Cal through the video lens, and Cal would remind Josh how he needed to eat before school. Noah was able to drive and even act as a surrogate for Josh at parent-teacher conferences, that were often required for Josh's bad behavior.

After getting dropped off at school, Josh would soon hear, "What's up, Nerd? Are you enjoying your day so far?" The voice was from Bub, a chubby friend of Josh's that always seemed to have an excuse to have a snack in his hand. His parents often would send him to school with carrots, but Bub had programmed his Noah to sneak snacks in his backpack every morning.

"Nothing Bub!" Josh replied as if he was annoyed by being called that by his friend every day.

"Where's Yashi and Terra?" Bub asked.

"I'm sure they are in Mrs. Taylor's class," Josh replied.

"I need to remind them that it's a big Moon Night," Bub said with excitement in his voice. Moon Night was a tradition of friends. On the nights that ProTech announced and released new updates to their software, the friends would ride their bicycles to a mountainside in Valley Hills and look at the city together. For Bub, this generally meant that it was an excuse for him to have snacks. Still, for the others, it came to represent an escape from the technology surrounding them. Some conversations ranged from who was the best superhero to the newest apps for their Noah's.

"Ok, I will see you there in a minute." Bub hurried away.

Josh stopped at his locker and noticed that across the hall, a new girl, he had never seen, walked to the set of lockers. She had flowing blonde hair with blue eyes. He was almost locked in a moment of staring when Tad Phillips came up and slammed his locker door with a sarcastic shout, "Wake up, Nunley!"

Tad Phillips was the quintessential jock at Valley Hills Middle School. He played, what seemed to be, every sport in the school and usually with great success. His father, Ned, was a marketing expert with ProTech, which meant that he didn't have the demands of life that Cal experienced and often was the coach of every one of Tad's teams. Dek Bale also gave his marketing experts the ability to sale features of AL-LIs that code had not been developed for as a way to meet the demands of people. Ned generally oversold on promises of the technology of AL-LIs that Cal was tasked with having to clean up his messes with the development of apps to meet the demands. This tension led to Ned having a strenuous and often complaintive attitude towards Cal that overflowed to Tad picking on Josh.

Josh, noticing that the new girl was watching the scene between Tad and Josh, tried to cover the embarrassment caused by Tad's bullying. "What do you want, Tad?" Josh tried to cover under his breath.

Tad said, "Nunley, we are going to the football field after school and need another person to make up the team. Are you in?"

Josh inquired hesitantly, "What's the angle, Tad?"

Tad, "No angle, just come."

Not wanting to look like he was backing down and realizing that more people were watching, especially the new girl, Josh looked confidently at Tad and said, "I'll be there!"

Josh slowly walked away from the conversation, realizing that he was not an athlete, much less a football player. Yet, as he was walking away, the new girl smiled for a moment and whispered, "Hi, I'm Ellie Grace." Josh's attitude changed. As he slipped into Mrs. Taylor's biology lab class, Yashi and Terra were already getting ready for the experiment of the day, while Bub was trying his new favorite pickup line with the girls in the class, which usually meant his rejection. The friends noticed something different about Josh. Yet Josh remained in a stare reflecting about what just happened in the hallway.

The bell rang to begin class, and Josh remained in a state of being zoned out. "Josh, Josh, JOSH!" Yashi said louder to get Josh's attention. "Hey man, you in zombie land or something?"

"What?" Josh said, halfway confused about where he was and what was happening around him.

"Oh, I have seen that stare before from him," Terra whispered.

"What stare?" Josh sharply replied.

"The stare about a girl," Terra said to the group.

Yashi's face lit up and said out loud, "A girl?"

"Shhh. Leave me alone. You don't know what you are talking about." Josh stated.

"What's going on?" Bub entered into the conversation at a regular tone of voice.

"Josh has a girl," Yashi whispered slowly.

"A girl? That's awesome, do you want some pickup lines?" Bub said. Then all of a sudden, from the front of the class, a voice rang out, "Mr. Brown." Bub straightened up in his seat and turned around. He hated

his last name being said out loud to the class as it always got a few chuckles.
"Your conversation is so good that you must share with all of us." Mrs. Taylor explained.
"Uhh, uhh, I'm sorry, Mrs. Taylor," Bub nervously said, searching for a comment like a pickup line. "I was helping Josh with a biology problem."
Mrs. Taylor rolled her eyes and said, "Ok, well, let's discuss our chapter today and not your personal biology content."
As she began to teach using augmented reality technology, Josh whispered to the others, "I think I have a bigger problem, I have been asked to play football with Tad after school." "What?" All three friends said in unison in shock as Mrs. Taylor stared at the group.
After class, all four were walking to their lockers when Bub began to chime in as he was eating a Twinkie, "Josh, you are not a football player. If I have learned anything in biology class, it is that you are scientifically unable to play football."
Yashi chimed in, "Yeah, man, I can't believe you agreed to play, especially with Tad, Mr. Football."
Right about that moment, the new girl, Ellie Grace, walked to her locker, gave Josh a quick smile, got her stuff, and walked to her next course. Josh was lost in what was being said around him.
"Josh!" Terra said to bring him back to reality, "Will Ellie Grace be there to watch?" she asked.
"Guys, I have no idea, I just want to play football," Josh moved quickly as he started to grab his books for his next class from his locker.
"Something sounds fishy," Yashi said.

"You are from Japan; everything sounds like fish and sushi to you, Yashi," Bub said. "Go for it, bro! Playing football could raise our street cred. But remember that we have Moon Night."

"Yeah, man, Moon Night tonight at 7 p.m.!" Terra chimed in. "And don't forget that this is a special Moon Night!"

"Ok, see you all there," Josh said as he tried to end the conversation quickly so he could focus on Ellie Grace, that was getting her things out of her locker as well.

Just that moment, Tad walked up and broke Josh's concentration on Ellie Grace and said, "Hey Nunley, we actually get to start playing football right at 2:30 p.m., so make sure you are on the field then. Deal?"

"Ok, I'll be there!" Josh said with an air of confidence.

Every day when school finished, Noah stood there waiting for Josh's arrival along with some of the other versions of AL-LIs. They didn't speak or interact with each other; rather, they stood in a line anticipating the arrival of their child. The AL-LIs would then guide them to a car or transport pod to bring them home.

Today, Josh walked to Noah and said, we are doing something different today. "Josh, I am not sure if this is to be approved by your father," Noah replied.

"Noah, I made a promise to be somewhere, and I need to be there," Josh countered. "And it will only take one hour, and it will replace my time that I usually play on my iPad at home."

"What are you going to do?" Noah asked.

"Play football," Josh said.

"Do I need to go and get your clothes to play in?" Noah asked.

"No, these clothes will be fine," Josh said.

It was after school, on the football field, and Josh found himself standing there alone. He could see that everyone was starting to get out of school. He looked down at his watch, wondering if he was at the right place and time. He even noticed Yashi, Terra, and Bub standing by the fence. Then all of a sudden, as if a flood of water and embarrassment were combined in a sound, the sprinklers came on the football field, and Josh realized at that moment that he had been pranked by Tad. Josh just stood there in shock and awe for a moment as he got soaked.

Then all of a sudden, he heard Tad yelling in front of all the people, "Hey Nunley, I forgot to tell you that we were going to play mud football, but I can see you already started." Not knowing what to do, Josh looked up and noticed what seemed like the whole school was watching him get soaked.

What hurt more than anything, was that Ellie Grace walked by with a group of girls and let out a gasp of laughter at Josh. Slowly, he began to walk to the fence where his friends were staring in sympathy as one stream after another of the sprinklers continued to hit his body.

"Do you want me to beat him up?" Terra said.

"Yeah, let me sick my AL-LI on him," Yashi said.

"I can put him in destruction mode," Bub said.

"No, guys, I'm going just to go home." Josh said as he hung his head.

"Hey man, what about Moon Night?" Bub asked.

"I don't know. I'm just not feeling it tonight." Josh said as he walked away.

And then there was Noah. His facial recognition technology allowed him to recognize moments of sadness. In an attempt to comfort, Noah held up his fingers to Josh and said, "Two of everything," as if hoping to get a response from Josh. Josh was so upset that he stormed by; he didn't put up his fingers and got in the car to go home. Noah waved at Josh's friends and said, "See you all tomorrow." The car drive home was silent.

Chapter 3

When Everything Changed

It was fourteen years ago when Cal and Deborah Nunley got word of ProTech's shift towards artificial intelligence they went to meet with Bale and shared their desire to develop the first artificial intelligence robot that demonstrated social and emotional intelligence. Bale realized that Cal and Deborah were the missing links in where his vision for ProTech had stalled. Bale soon released to the company the creation of the research and development section of ProTech headed by Cal and Deborah. Thus, Cal and Deborah began their journey working with Bale.

Cal and Deborah were a part of the original team, called the Alpha Team when the code for AL-LIs was developed along with James Newton and Jezzie Ahabin. As they realized the innovation of AL-LIs, they sought a way to provide this type of interaction with humans in the form of a humanistic robot. Noah became the teams crowning achievement. Their years of hard work came together in fruition with Noah's development, and with Cal and Deborah's lead, they were awarded Noah as a prototype to see how he would do in home environments. The team, along with Bale, would gather at Cal and Deborah's house to do round-robins of tests using apps for Noah. Some of the tests went well, and some not so well. The team always joked, in particular, there was the one test of cooking that happened, and Noah couldn't read the bar code scanner that Jezzie developed for food products, so the homemade chicken pot pie ended up in the trash after the first bite. One of the original agreements of the Noah team was to ensure that the ethical line was firmly established and never crossed regarding the use of Noah's technology. Anything promoting violence or abuse of any kind was considered off-hands for the Alpha Team.

Soon Cal and Deborah decided they were ready to have a child. Thirteen years ago, they got pregnant with Josh and began to make their plans for their family to begin. They were in their 38th week of pregnancy and still working at ProTech each day in preparation for the release of more AL-LI technology.

Each developer, including Bale, would spend private time with Noah working and testing different innovations and prototype apps to be used with Noah. One night, in particular, the Alpha Team had left to celebrate Noah's new innovation of being able to detect humans within a 50-foot distance, which was to be used as a security measure for Noah. Bale dismissed himself from going to the celebration and told the team he wanted to do some more work with Noah.

As the team was walking out of the building, Deborah forgot the fab to her car and told Cal that it would only take a moment to run back upstairs to get it. She said how the extra steps would help prepare her for delivery. Cal told the team to go ahead to the customary restaurant and get their usual table and that he would wait for Deborah at the bottom floor.

As Deborah returned to the Alpha Team floor, she could hear Bale's 90's hip-hop music blaring from the testing room that was blacked out to prevent anyone from seeing in the room to protect the confidentiality of the testing. She smiled to herself as she went to her workstation to get her fab, but she noticed that the door was cracked. As she walked by, hoping to catch a glimpse of Bale dancing or rapping, all she could see was Noah. It had in its hand two guns and was standing in a ready to fire position. She could also see the expression of anger on Noah's face that had not been previously programmed to occur.

Deborah was confused as she had never seen Noah look that way and was confused as to the whereabouts of Bale. Suddenly, Noah turned towards the door, stared at Deborah, and said out loud, "Sir, we are not alone, I can sense someone is there." As he held up his guns towards Deborah, the door swung open, and Bale looked in shock to see Deborah standing at the doorway, in shock as well.

"What are you doing here?" Bale yelled at Deborah.

"What am *I* doing here? What are *you* doing, Dek? Why does Noah look like this? What is he doing?"

Bale stepped out in the hall, pushing Deborah back, and quickly closed the door behind him and exclaimed, "You need to leave right now!"

"Dek, what is your plan with Noah?" Deborah asked hesitantly.

Bale responded sharply, "I don't have to explain myself or my actions to you! I own you! I own all of you! And if you tell anyone of what you saw, you will be in breach of your confidentiality, even with Cal. So, I suggest that you leave and never speak again about what you saw or else."

Deborah, "Or else what?"

Bale whispered back sharply, "Do you want to find out what I am capable of?" Do you?" As he began to rub her belly.

Deborah immediately pulled back, in awe of what she was hearing.

As she drifted away, Bale stared at her to make sure that she left. As the elevator's door shut, Deborah could hear the music begin to play again. As the elevator reached the bottom floor, she realized that she would have to compose herself before seeing Cal not to raise any questions about what happened. When she got off the elevator and saw Cal, she knew she wasn't in the mood to celebrate, so she told Cal to take her home as she was not feeling well.

Meanwhile, Bale called his head of security, Broderick, and simply said, "Deborah knows too much, she must be taken care of." To which Broderick replied, "Yes, sir."

As Cal and Deborah were standing at the front of Pro-Tech waiting for their car to come and pick them up, Deborah began to feel nervous. "Cal?" she said with a quiver in her voice. "Yes, Deb," Cal replied. "Do you ever feel like we are being watched here at ProTech?" Deborah asked as she looked around.

"What do you mean?" Cal replied. "Of course, we do! That's why there are a million cameras everywhere on the property."

"No, I mean, do you ever feel like it's only us that are being watched as developers.?" Deborah asked even more nervously.

Cal, taken back by her questions at first, tried to lighten the mood. He embraced Deborah and said, "Honey, you know that this place is just like the ever-watching eye in Lord of the Rings. It's always there watching us." As Cal embraced Deborah even more, he then began to look up towards Bale's high-rise office that stood above Valley Hills. "He's always watching us. He may even be watching us now." Cal leaned over and kissed Deborah's neck.

"I'm serious, Cal!" Deborah replied.

"Me too!" as Cal tried to kiss Deborah again, to which she pushed him away.

Deborah stated, "It seems like the car is taking forever to get here."

Cal replied, "Yeah, maybe something happened in the garage."

About that time, the car arrived. As they were getting into the car, Deborah looked back over her shoulder. She could see Broderick emerging from the garage. But she never said anything to Cal.

As they were heading home, Cal and Deborah began to drift asleep as the car turned along Outer Hills Dr. The car slowly began to speed up along the winding road that ran along with the outermost parts of Valley Hills. Deborah woke all of a sudden to realize that the car was speeding excessively along the roads. "Cal wake up!" she yelled as Cal tried to grab the wheel to take control. However, as they reached, Bender's Curve, Cal for a moment regained control. However, he overcorrected the steering wheel. The car then began to slide and went off the curve and headed towards the deep ravine, where a severe crash occurred, taking the life of Deborah yet sparing Cal and eventually Josh.

In the hospital, Cal woke to the presence of Dek Bale and Broderick in his room.

"Should I get the nurse?" Broderick asked.

"No, let's wait and have some time with Cal," Bale replied.

"How are you feeling? Cal?" Bale asked.

"I'm not sure...what happened?" Cal confusingly replied.

"You had an accident at Bender's Curve," Bale said. "Your car had a malfunction, and you were speeding along Outer Hills Dr. It's sad to see when technology has these glitches. Do you know what a glitch is, Cal?"

Cal, confused at the question and wondering about Deborah and Josh asked, "Glitch? Glitch? What do you mean, a glitch? Where are Deborah and Josh? I need to see them."

"Did Deborah ever mention about a glitch that night?" Bale asked.

"What? No! What glitch?" Cal said confusingly.

"Sir, it's time." Broderick interrupted.

"Shhh," Bale tried to speak calmly to Cal. "Josh is totally fine, and that is all that you need to know right now."

"What about Deborah?" Cal exclaimed.

"Sleep is all you need right now," Bale eerily said to Cal.

At that moment, Cal could see Broderick put a needle into his port of his IV and inject a substance, and Cal slowly began to sleep.

When Cal woke up, the nurse tending to him, immediately got on her radio and said, "Get Dr. Randu to come immediately. Mr. Nunley is awake."

Cal slowly began to say, "Where are Deborah and Josh? I need to see them."

The nurse replied, "Dr. Randu will be able to help you when he gets here."

Dr. Randu hurried into the room. "Mr. Nunley, it's great to see you are awake."

Cal angrily looked at the doctor. "I need to see my wife and son. Where are they?"

Dr. Randu immediately asked, "You mean you don't know?"

"Know what?" Cal said with even more anger.

"Cal," Dr. Randu continued, "During the accident, Deborah suffered many injuries. We did all that we could do, but we weren't able to save her life."

Cal began to sob and asked, "And what about the baby?"

"Well, he was close enough to the delivery date that we had to go ahead and deliver him." Dr. Randu continued, "But he is fine and a healthy baby boy. Mr. Dek Bale said that you guys wanted to name him Joshua."

At that moment, one of the nurses pushed a cart into the room that had Josh swaddled inside it. "Here he is!" one of the nurses exclaimed. "Sweet little Joshua."

"This is the first time I can remember ever seeing Mr. Bale being this involved with a family." Dr. Randu stated to Cal.

"What do you mean?" Cal asked.

"Oh, you must not know?" Dr. Randu stated, "Dek Bale has covered all your medical bills for the accident, birth, and provided a $10,000,000 life insurance policy for the death of Deborah." Cal stared off into the distance, trying to take in the range of emotions with the death of Deborah, the birth of Joshua, and the question of Bale's involvement.

A few days later, Dek Bale stood beside Cal at Deborah's funeral service and even asked Cal if he could provide a eulogy at the service. When Cal tried to address the crowd, he was overwhelmed with his grief and couldn't even speak, and Bale stepped forward to comfort him. After the service, Cal retreated to his house with Josh and found there were friends and family gathered. Upon entering the house, Cal's sister, Abby, started to give directions for everyone to eat. Cal said softly to Abby, "I really just want to be alone with Josh." Abby replied in disbelief, "What?"

Cal then blurted out, "I really want everyone to leave. I just want to be alone with Josh."

Abby stepped forward to try and guide Cal to change his tone, but he pulled away fiercely and said to everyone, "It's time to go!"

Abby stood outside, apologizing to the crowd as they left. When she walked back inside, she found Cal in their bedroom, gazing at the pictures that were on their dresser. All of a sudden, with a violent swipe of his arm, he knocked over some of the photos and began to sob. Abby came into the room and tried to hug him, and Cal pulled away again and yelled, "Just leave me alone."

Abby stood back and said, "Cal, I am here to help you. Your friends are here to help you. We know this is difficult. We hate that this happened. But remember that you have a sweet baby boy that needs a father. I can't fix what happened in the past, but I can be here to help you go forward in the future. I am praying for you, Cal."

"Prayer?" Cal shouted. "Prayer? Who am I to pray to? Where is a god during this time?"

Abby replied, "Cal, I am not sure what you guys do here at Valley Hills, but the reality is that there is a God that loves you very much. He loves you, Josh, and Deborah. And He wants to help you through this time. But He isn't going to force you to take those steps. He is going to love you in this mess of your life and help you." Abby returned to the kitchen and collected her purse and began to leave.

"Abby!" Cal replied, "I am sorry! Thank you for helping me during this time. I am sorry for taking my anger out on you."

Abby hugged Cal and said, "I understand, and God understands. Take care of that boy!"

Chapter 4

A Reset Begins

Josh stormed into the house, ran upstairs, slammed the door, and threw his backpack across his room, and fell on his bed sobbing. He didn't care that his clothes were sopping wet. He was too angry and embarrassed to care. "How could I let this happen?" He said out loud. "I am such an idiot." He said again. He had a small punching bag in his room hanging from the ceiling, and he started to hit the bag without any gloves. The more and more he hit the bag, the angrier he got, and the more he cried.
Then suddenly, there was a knock at the door.
"Go away, Noah. I am ok." Josh yelled.
"Josh," Noah softly replied. "I have your father on, and he wants to speak to you."
"I don't want to talk to him," Josh said as he hit the bag some more.
"Son!" Cal said through Noah. "What happened?"

"Nothing, dad!" Josh sharply replied. "I just got a little wet."
"Noah told me what happened, and I am sorry," Cal said.
Josh replied, "Well, if I wasn't such a dork with a robot, I would have known about how to play football, Cal." Josh knew that when he used Cal's name, it made him upset because he knew it made him feel distant.
"Son! I have told you before…" Cal tried to reply.
"Told me what?" Josh retorted. "Told me to do what? You have never told me anything. All you have told me is what Noah has told me. You haven't said anything to me, ever. And you aren't saying anything to me now." In a swift action, Josh was able to shut off the conversation with Cal through Noah's eyes.
Noah had seen Josh this upset before, and rather than seeking to reach out to Cal again, he stood there with Josh. Josh looked at Noah and said, "He has never said anything to me. Never!" And slowly, Josh began to sob and fell into the arms of Noah. Noah was programmed in these moments to provide an embrace to Josh.
As Josh slipped back into his room, Noah called Cal again. "Josh is in his room and will be ok, sir."
"Ok, I understand," Cal replied.
"Sir, I must ask, did you forget about today?" Noah asked.
"What?" Cal said.
"It is Josh's birthday. How do you want me to proceed?"
"Oh no! I forgot completely. I have been caught up in so much here." Cal said. "Make sure that the pizza has whatever he wants on it. I'll see about getting a gift on my way home."

"Yes, sir!" Noah replied. "Don't forget that tonight is also your release night."

Cal replied strongly, "I know that Noah, I don't have to be reminded of how important tonight is."

"Yes, sir!" Noah replied as they disconnected.

The release of ProTech's newest upgrade was set to occur at 6 p.m. that night. The buzz was all around Valley Hills as watch parties were being arranged around the campus of ProTech and in the city. Bale was planning a special announcement and launch at 6 p.m. that evening. He was flying in celebrities from around the world that made it one of the most sought-after events to attend. He even provided a hologram concert of some of the most memorable bands within the last century.

Upgrade events were generally bittersweet for Cal and Josh. Cal was required to be in the office to ensure that all the technology worked smoothly as well as to meet investors and potential investors in ProTech. However, Josh often was forced to be at home being watched by Noah. Upgrade nights for Josh often meant that Cal would get pizza delivered. Still, with the amount of activity going on in Valley Hills, it often arrived late and cold.

The event was live-streamed across all devices in Valley Hills as a way to promote Bale's branding of ProTech. However, the events always featured a sense of secrecy as even some of ProTech's designers were unaware of what the final releases all entailed. Bale enjoyed this aspect of secrecy as it gave him ultimate ownership of the products going out to the people as well as protection from any news outlets getting information prior to the release.

However, for some reason, this release was not like prior ones. Bale seemed to be going over-the-top on the promotion and stating how this was to be the biggest innovation yet. For Cal and the Alpha team, they scoured over the codes and updates to ensure that they aligned, especially right before Bale made his announcement. The window to look over the codes had gotten smaller and smaller, and often Broderick and his team watched over the developer team to ensure there was no outside contact regarding the release.

Following Deborah's death, Bale personally selected a team member named Zerah to replace her. Zerah soon became Bale's girlfriend. Her presence changed the dynamic of the team as Bale seemed to be influenced now by Zerah instead of each person feeling like they could offer their input. Their relationship seemed to be very toxic, and inside jokes were often made among the rest of the team, sometimes just to get Zerah jealous towards Bale. Soon, it became evident with Cal, Jezzie, and James, that Zerah was hired more for her looks rather than her skills. She barely had any coding experience. When it came to updates that required the team to review update codes to be released, Zerah often spent more time preparing for the update parties than reviewing the codes.

On the night of update releases, the Alpha team would be in their office where their cubicles formed a crosshair formation in the middle of the room. Most of the time, the team would receive the codes three-to-four hours early as Bale put his final touches on the code. For Cal and the team, it was always interesting to see what codes would arrive and what updates would be involved as their work culminated together in this moment of realization. Often, the practice was to not review your own codes but the codes of everyone else. Broderick and the security team would stand guard to ensure that the team members would not be able to release any information to the press before the updates went out at 6 p.m.

On this night, it was 4:30 p.m., and the Alpha team had yet to receive the newest update code package. They were waiting up in their offices, when all of a sudden Broderick and his team burst into the room and said, "The updated code is ready." He would then go over to the centralized computer that held all their updates and work to ensure that the codes could not be taken from ProTech to other companies. He would then enter a special security code that would unlock the programming code for the Alpha Team to begin their review.

Usually, the team would meticulously begin to go through the entire code. However, tonight Broderick seemed to be more hesitant. He pushed towards their work to be completed quickly already with a smaller window to complete the update review. After the first few minutes, Jezzie looked up at Broderick and said, "I need to go to the bathroom." Since this was totally out of character during a code review to have a team member to leave the group, it caught Broderick and the other members of the team off guard. He went to a corner to make a phone call. While Broderick was turned away, Jezzie looked at Cal and whispered, "I need to talk to you. Now!"

Broderick returned and said that Bale was fine with Jezzie going to the restroom. Cal then spoke up and said, "Can I go as well? We both ate Indian today, and it is not sitting with me either?" Frustrated by their

request, Broderick replied, "Seriously, Nunley!" Rather than stopping the progress, Broderick motioned for them both to go. "Both of you keep reviewing the code," Broderick voiced towards James and Zerah. Broderick then turned to one of his security guards and barked, "Follow them to the door; make sure they don't leave."
As Cal went into the restroom, he was immediately met by Jezzie. "Did you see it?"
"Did I see what?" Cal replied.
"The code. The glitch in the code." Jezzie said.
"Are you sure? There has never been a glitch in the code." Cal said.
"Cal, the glitch was in your code," Jezzie replied.
"My code? I have never had a glitch in my code." Cal replied.
"I know," Jezzie said. "Something is up. Are you sure you didn't accidentally input a glitch?"
"Jezzie, I promise I didn't put in a glitch," Cal said. "How did it get in there?"
"I don't know, but I am scared that everyone else is going to see it in there, and I wanted you to be aware because it is serious."
"How serious?" Cal asked.
Jezzie slowed down and looked at Cal intently, "The glitch that I saw was reverse zombie code."
"How is that possible? Everyone knows that reverse zombie code is impossible." Cal replied. Zombie code was a way for a code to be applied to the AL-Lis that, if enacted, would bring about the destruction of the AL-LI based upon a certain action or response. However, reverse zombie code, worked from the AL-LIs learning how to maintain their survival during a time of destruction, thus entering

into a zombie state and destroying everything else. Ethically, it was a code that meant the survival of the machine over humans, which went against all that the Alpha team agreed to in their work.

Jezzie began to pace around and say out loud, "What are we going to do when we get back to the room? Everyone is going to have seen it. We need a plan. We need to get you out of here."

Cal replied, "Why can't I just go in there and delete the code and remove the glitch?"

"It will be too obvious if you remove it, and it will cause even more questions," Jezzie said.

"Yeah, but if I leave, won't there be even more questions?" said Cal.

"Yes, but at least you can blame about being sick," said Jezzie. "Then, let me see about covering for you with the rest of the team."

About that time, a huge bang on the door. It was Broderick. "Hey, let's hurry it up. We have more code to review."

Jezzie hollered out, "Just a minute." Then he grabbed Cal and told him to splash some water on his face and shirt to make it look like he was sweating.

Jezzie went to the door and barely opened it, "Cal isn't feeling well. The food got to him more than to me. He asked if I would pick up his work. I am fine to do it. He really needs to go home."

Broderick replied, "I will need to check with Bale." As he was about to pick up his phone, Cal threw open the door and immediately vomited on Broderick's shoes.

Horrified, Broderick said, "Get out of here, man. Don't get anyone else sick."

As Caleb rushed out to the elevator, he looked back, and Jezzie nodded to affirm their plan.

On the ride down, the questions and confusion began to overwhelm Caleb to the point that he actually vomited again in the elevator. He knew that he couldn't immediately go home as he was fearful of what was to come. He made a stop at his favorite store and took off on Outer Hills Road again.

When Cal finally left, Jezzie came back to the team room met with very confused looks by James and Zerah. Jezzie tried to look at James to let him know something was going on, but he had to try and be aware of Broderick and his team's suspicion.

"Where's Cal?" Zerah asked.

"Oh, he's going home, he's not feeling well," Jezzie replied. "I am going to cover him for this one."

During this time, Broderick was in the corner again, making a phone call. Bale could be heard on the other line, "Get him back here now! He is the key. Even if you have to track him down, GET HIM BACK NOW!"

"Yes, sir!" Broderick's replied as he stormed out of the room. He looked back at one of his men and said, "Make sure no one leaves until they have reviewed all the code! They only have 30 minutes before we go live!"

About this time, Jezzie looked at James as if to say, follow along.

Jezzie then looked at Zerah, "Did you see all the celebrities that are here? I think I saw a bunch of beautiful models.

James then chimed in, "Wonder what they are doing right now with Bale? Aren't they all having a dance celebration party?"

"I'm not thinking about that, Jezzie," Zerah replied.

"Oh, I know you are not thinking about it," Jezzie said. "I'm just wondering if Bale is thinking about you."

Zerah then slammed her hands on the table and yelled, "That's it!" She ferociously went over to Broderick's men and said, "I want to see Dek right now! While I am down here doing this boring stuff, he is up there with who knows! Take me up there now!"

"Ms. Zerah, we have been given orders." One of the men replied.

'Forget your orders; take me to Dek!" Zerah replied. Zerah and the men continued to argue.

Jezzie then looked at James and said, "Hey, Cal didn't write the reverse zombie code!"

James replied, "I saw it, and I was scared to say anything at first because I knew he wouldn't have done that. What do we do?"

Jezzie said, "We have to let it go through, but we have to trace the code."

James said, "We can run a history of the code that will show who worked on it when, but it will take a little bit to get it done."

Jezzie asked, "How much time do you need?"

James said, "Considering this code, forty-five minutes at least."

Jezzie said, "Well, you have thirty. I will review the rest of the code."

"Ok, but you know that Bale will know afterward that we did this," James said, and he got a disk from his desk and began to run a trace while they were arguing.

"We can't worry about that right now. We have to protect Cal." Jezzie replied.

Chapter 5

Home Security

Often on the night of updates, AL-LIs would go to a specific station and stand on a pod in their house or work. The release would automatically occur simultaneously for all AL-LIs. The period that the AL-LIs were being programmed became known as the Stone Age, as all technology seemed to stop for a moment in the city. For Josh, Bub, Yashi, and Terra, the Stone Age period became the perfect excuse for Moon Night to occur, but tonight was different for Josh. Upset at his father for forgetting his birthday and not being present, Josh was sitting in his room watching videos from ProTech's video service, Spot-On. It was just a few moments before 6 p.m. when Josh heard a light knock on his door.
Noah came into the room and sat down on the end of Josh's bed, looking as fatherly as he could. "Josh," Noah began. "You know that I am about to go on the pod to get my update. Just in case there is

something that happens that erases my memory, which I know there never is, I just want to tell you it has been an extreme pleasure to be your Al-LI." Josh, at first, was resistant to Noah as it made this speech every time to Josh before his updates occurred. Noah then looked at Josh and spoke almost with emotion, "I want you to know that your dad loves you, and I am proud of you, Josh." At that moment, Josh was overwhelmed with emotion and went over to Noah and gave him a big hug. They pulled away, and Noah held up his two fingers, "Two of everything?" Josh smiled and said, "Two of everything, Noah."

"Well, it's time," Noah said as he began his way down to his pod. Josh just stared at Noah as he went down the stairs. Understanding in this moment how he was both an artificial intelligence robot and a friend. Noah then went to his pod and stood at attention, and the light in his eyes seemed to dim as he stood there with small flashes going through his eyes every so often.

All of a sudden, Josh heard something like a small rock hit his window. He looked outside and saw Bub, Yashi, and Terra standing there beside their bikes. Josh motioned that he would be down in a minute. When he went outside, Bub said, "Hey, bro! Come on, last chance, it's your birthday Moon Night."

"Not this time, guys," Josh replied, slightly disappointed, "For some reason, I just feel that I need to be here tonight."

"Are you ok?" Terra asked.

"Yeah, are you thinking about that girl?" Yashi asked.

"Yeah, man, do you want a snack?" Bub replied.

"No, guys, I want to wait up for my dad tonight," Josh said.

They knew that it was a terrible excuse, but they also knew it was not worth the battle. Josh turned to go back inside. Terra and Yashi began to ride off. Bub stood there for a moment, looking at Josh. "Come on, Bub, hurry up." Yashi yelled out. Bub slowly turned to his bike and began to catch up with the rest.

Josh went back inside and went to his room and fell asleep.

A little later, Josh woke up and went to the bathroom and then decided to go downstairs to check on Noah and to see if his dad had not come home. He looked outside and noticed that his dad's vehicle wasn't home yet, which was weird as his dad generally came home early on the nights of updates. He also noticed that Noah was still standing on his pod. He looked at his watch and noticed that the time was around 9 p.m., which was very unusual for an update to last this long. Generally, the Stone Age period was around two hours. At first, he just left Noah there as his pod was close to the kitchen. Suddenly, Josh could hear a commotion outside. He noticed that different police cars were going down the street, more than usual. He could also hear different helicopters flying overhead with spotlights going. Something must have been going on. He reached into the fridge to get his favorite drink and sat down at the table.

He turned on his Home Screen and began to see a news flash coming across Spot On. Josh focused his attention on the broadcaster's voice, "It can now be confirmed that ProTech almost suffered an extreme glitch tonight in their update. The glitch was set to cause several ALLIs to go into what is being called destructive mode against their owners, which was intended to bring about the death of some of ProTech's employees." The broadcaster paused for a moment and looked away and then returned, "It has just come to our attention that the ones responsible for this glitch are none other than Cal Nunley and James Newton of the Alpha Team, some of the original developers of AL-LIs. Fortunately, Dek Bale was able to catch the glitch at the last moment and change the update. However, it is unsure if all AL-Lis have been impacted by the update. Be aware that you need to ask your AL-LI to go to their pods for their updates before letting them resume their duties. If you have any information leading to the capture of Cal Nunley or James Newton, please let the authorities know immediately."

Josh was stunned at what he heard. He couldn't believe that his own father was being accused of the glitch. He began to hear more police cars driving by. Then he looked back at Noah, but he wasn't there. Then all of a sudden, from out of nowhere, Noah grabbed Josh and slung him across the room on the floor. Josh tried to gather himself and scurry away. He began to scream at Noah. "Noah, stop! Noah, it's me, Josh." Yet Noah began throwing chairs and the table out of the way. Josh didn't know what to do. He ran upstairs to a closet to try and hide. He tried to sit there as silent as possible. But then Noah's arm burst through the wood door and began to tear down the door. Noah's arm got stuck for a moment, and Josh tried to escape again and ran downstairs. As he ran, he tried to pull whatever he could find to be an obstacle to Noah. He tried to hide underneath the dining room table. But as Noah came down, he knew where he was, and he lifted the table on one end and tried to slam it down on top of Josh. Josh scurried away to the kitchen, where he grabbed his drink and threw it at Noah, which the liquid caused Noah to pause for a moment. Noah stopped and shook its head. Josh realized there was nowhere else for him to go. He was trapped in the kitchen. There was nothing else for him to do. He simply looked at Noah and then screamed while turning his head, preparing for what may come next, "Noah, two of everything" and held up his fingers.

Nothing happened. Josh looked at Noah. And he had stopped and was staring at Noah's fingers, almost examining them as a doctor. He reached up and began to touch the fingers in almost a trance. He then paused and slowly moved his hand next to Josh's in the same formation and whispered, "Two of everything."

Noah looked at Josh, in a moment of gathering its consciousness and asked, "What happened?"

"You almost killed me!" Josh said.

"What?" Noah replied with confusion and fear, "I almost killed you! Oh, Josh, I am so sorry. Something must have happened with the update."

"Wait, you remember me before the update?" Josh asked, as well.

"Yes! Of course, I remember you." Noah replied. "I just don't know what happened to me. All I know is that I started to feel wet, and then my system began to restore. I saw your fingers and my system fully reset."

Noah paused for a moment, "Josh, I am getting the news now about your father. They are looking for him, which means they are going to come here."

"What did my father do?" Josh asked.

"I don't know, but I know they are going to come here," Noah said.

"What do I need to do?" Josh started to get more nervous.

"Hold on. I am getting something from your father." Noah said.

All of a sudden, Cal's voice began to play through Noah. "Josh, you have to understand that James and I did not do this. I cannot say where I am right now, but you need to find your aunt Abby. She will be able to help you. She is a protector. Noah, destroy this message after Josh sees it."

"Yes, sir," Noah replied as his eyes flashed.

"Wait, Dad!" Josh yelled out. "Noah, bring him back. Where is he? How will I find Aunt Abby?"

Suddenly, there was a hard banging on the door.

"Mr. Nunley, it is the police. We need you and your AL-LI to come with us. We have some questions."

Noah motioned for Josh to go and hide. "Remember to find Abby, no matter what happens to me."

Josh hid in a hallway closet and was able to see through the door barely. Noah went to the front door and opened it. The police burst in and grabbed Noah and said, "Where is Mr. Nunley?"

Josh noticed that the chief walked in. He looked at one of the officers and said, "Be careful of the glitch. He could still have it. Hook him up and scan him."

All of a sudden, one of the officers put a cord into Noah's port on the back of his neck.

"Mr. Nunley is not here. I am unaware of his current location. I can tell you that without having to scan me." Noah replied.

"Be quiet AL-LI, we will know soon enough." The officer said.

Suddenly, one of the officers hit the other and motioned towards the outside and said, "Look, he's here."

Josh tried to look further out the door without being noticed, but he couldn't see anything.

All of a sudden, Broderick and Dek Bale walked in, and the chief said, "Mr. Bale, Nunley is not here, and this is his AL-LI. He says he doesn't know of his current location."

Dek Bale was at Josh's house. He couldn't believe it and was confused about why he was there.

Bale then said to Broderick, "Take Noah to my office at ProTech, I will evaluate him personally." Then turning to the chief, he asked, "And what about the boy?"

One of the officers that had been looking around said, "No sign of him here."

"He will show up, I'm sure. Keep an officer outside to watch over the house and begin to scan the property after I leave." Bale said.

"Yes sir!" the officers replied almost in unison.

Bale then looked at Noah and almost snarled as he said, "You don't know his location? Or you don't want to say? I will find out. For now, paralyze him."

Josh knew enough that paralyzing was a form of arrest for an AL-LI. The officers began to treat him harshly and pushed him down on the ground. The way that Noah landed, he was able to look towards Josh in the closet and shook his head, almost to say, don't do anything. Then they wrapped up his arms and put a cord to his port, his eyes flashed, and the officers ran the app that paralyzed Noah. It basically made Noah obey their every command while maintaining his stored memory.

When the commotion stopped, Josh knew that he had a limited time to getaway. He slowly peeked his head out the door and checked to make sure there wasn't anyone immediately in the house. He thought that he had to get to his bike that leaned outside on the fence, but he didn't know if there would be officers out the back.

He went upstairs to his window to look out at all the commotion. He could see many different police cars and even what seemed like more helicopters flying around his house. Now and then a light would scan the perimeter of his house, so he had to stay close to the floor. He grabbed his jacket and phone and then thought that the only way he could see out the back of the house was through the No-No room.

As he slowly slipped into the No-Go room, a light scanning the perimeter seemed to flash right into the windows. As Josh slid across the floor, he could look and see how there were two police officers stationed out the back looking down the streets. He knew that he was going to have to have a distraction. So, he called Bub. "Come on, Bub, pick up."

Bub picked up and immediately began to shout. "Josh, it is like World War III out here in Valley Hills."

"Where are you?" Josh asked.

"We are out here at Moon Light. All I am seeing is police and helicopters. My dad called me and told me to stay away. What is going on?" Bub replied.

"Put me on speaker," Josh told Bub. "Ok, go for it," Bub replied.

"Guys, I don't know what is going on, and I can't explain it right now, but I need your help. I am stuck in my house, and I need a distraction to get my bike and get away. Will you come and help me?

"Why don't I just call my parents to come and get you?" Terra asked.
"No! They have to stay away from my house because they will know you are connected to me." Josh replied.
"Ok, we will be there!" Bub replied, almost heroically. "When you hear the eagle sound, you will know the coast is clear."
"Ok, but hurry," Josh said as he hung up. He sat there, confused about what all had happened in the last few moments. Where was his dad? Why was he involved? What was the glitch? Why was he supposed to see his Aunt Abby?
Josh then began to move out of the room, when the twinkling of something on a dresser caught his attention. It was the necklace with the special metal piece that looked like a cross. It was draped over a picture of Cal and Deborah when they were pregnant with Josh. The writing on the picture said, "Our special project- Joshua." Josh had never noticed his father smiling like that before. He was caught staring for a moment at the picture and looking at the necklace. He then noticed a picture of his Aunt Abby, standing beside a lighthouse in the background. Josh thought that maybe this is where I can find Aunt Abby when suddenly one of the lights scanning the perimeter flashed across the room. He dropped down to the floor. But before he left, he reached back up and grabbed the necklace and put it around his neck. He went back up to his bedroom to look for Noah. He was sitting in Broderick's car. Broderick was speaking with the chief about something that Josh couldn't understand. Still, the way it looked; Broderick was giving orders to the chief. He then got into his car, and it began to drive away.

The chief then turned away after he left and looked down towards the ground and shook his head in almost disbelief in what he heard. He then looked at the phone in his pocket and answered it and listened for a moment and then replied. "Yes sir, we will check it out." When he got off the phone, he began motioning towards the house, and Josh could hear him say to one of the officers, "Activity was just reported as being in the house, and as Broderick said, any means necessary to bring him in."
"Who?" The officer said.
"The boy is still here!" The chief said.
Suddenly, piercing through all the commotion, Josh could hear some sounds in the back of the house. He ran to the No-Go room and could see the officers running down the street away from the back of the house. Then there rung out across all the sounds a loud eagle cry in the opposite direction. Josh knew this had to be Bub. It was also perfect timing as the officers began to discuss how to come back into the house. Josh scurried down the stairs and could see the lights beginning to scan the front of the house where the officers had previously entered. He dashed the backdoor and slowly began to open it.
He heard the eagle cry again from Bub, which began to sound more like a blackbird than an eagle. He looked, and none of the officers were present in the back, and his bike was right there ready to go. Suddenly he heard from inside the house. "It looks like someone is going out the back." Josh grabbed his bike and began to ride down the street towards where the sound of the bird sounds was coming from. He realized that it was just outside of Tad's house. So Josh pulled up there and then heard a whisper, "Hey, this way."

It was Bub. And he motioned for Josh to come into Tad's garage. Reluctant at first, Josh went into the garage to find Bub, Yashi, and Terra. Confused, Josh asked, "Why are we here at Tad's house?"
"It was his idea," Yashi replied.
"His idea! What do you mean? It was his idea?" Josh asked, even more confused.
Bub spoke up. "When we pulled up and began to think of how to distract the officers, Tad saw us outside his house. And with a little motivation, we encouraged him to help us." Bub said as he looked towards Terra.
"What did you do?" Josh asked.
As he asked that, all of a sudden, Tad burst into the room. "Is he okay?" Tad asked.
"Yeah, he is. Thanks for your help." Yashi said.
Josh noticed that Tad's eye was swollen shut and blackened.
"Luckily, those officers are not fast runners. They must eat a bunch of donuts." Tad said, almost bragging.
Rather than addressing their prior history, Josh stood up and addressed the group, "Guys, they have taken Noah, and they believe that my father is responsible for everything that happened tonight. My father sent me a message before they got Noah saying that I need to find Aunt Abby, that she would help me. She is a protector."
"A Protector?" Yashi asked.
"Yeah, I don't know what that means, but I have to find her," Josh said.
"So, where is she?" Terra asked.

"I don't know. She left twelve years ago, when I was born, and I haven't seen her since. The only picture that I have is of her besides this lighthouse." Josh said.

"So, what do you want to do?" Bub asked.

"I need to get to Aunt Abby," Josh said.

"You mean, we need to get to Aunt Abby," Bub said.

"No, guys, there is no way that I can ask you all to do this. It's too dangerous." Josh said.

"Hey, we are already in this together," Bub said.

Tad then spoke up, "You mean to tell me that we have a fugitive of ProTech and Valley Hills in my garage, and I am supposed to find a way to help him escape from this city with all the cameras everywhere?"

Terra then made a fist and stood firm and said, "Yes, that is what we do for our friends."

Tad then said almost in a means of obedience, "Ok! But where are you going?"

Josh replied, "I don't know! All I have is this picture."

Tad said, "Wait a second. My dad used to collect books about lighthouses. Let me see where they are."

He slipped into his house.

Josh looked at Terra and said, "You motivated him?"

"Well, he hurt our friend; I wasn't going to let it happen to you again. Anyways, who wants to say that they got a black eye by a girl, especially Tad?"

The group could hear his father saying, "What in the world is all that commotion about, and how did you get a black eye?"

"Nothing, dad!" as Tad came back into the garage. "Here it is, I think this can help."
Yashi grabbed the book and looked through it and then said, "Let me see! Look there it is Point Arena Lighthouse. And it's in the next town over."
Bub stood and said, "Well, that's where we have to go."
But then Terra said, "How are we going to get there?"
"I'm not sure right now," Josh replied. "But we first of all have to figure out how to get out of ProTech. I am sure the cameras are all looking for me."
Bub then spoke up, "I got it! Barry!"
"Oh no, not Barry!" Yashi replied.
"Who is Barry?" Tad asked.
"Barry is Bub's older brother. He has the Spot-On channel "Adventures with Barry," where he streams through his lens's different adventures, which end up being more failures. He is always looking for the next "big thing," and yet I think he works part-time for ProTech, I think, in their landscape division." Terra replied.
"Temporarily," Bub said in defense of his brother. "And anyway, Barry has a van, and he owes me a favor."
Josh then spoke up, "Hey, we can't argue about this anymore. The more we wait here, arguing is the time that we need to be looking for my dad and Noah. Bub call Barry now."
Bub stepped to the corner of the garage, and the group could hear his conversation, "Barry...Barry...what do you mean who is this? This is your brother, look at your caller ID. Hey, I need you to come to give me a ride...No I am not with mom and dad...Come and get me at 35

Bluebird Cove now…Remember dude; you owed me for last month when you got caught! Stop what you are doing now and come and get your brother! I am texting you the address! Bye, love you too!"

Bub turned around, slightly embarrassed, and said, "He's coming."

As the group began to wait for Barry, Tad noticed that Josh was sitting by himself. He walked over and said, "Hey, man! I am really sorry this all happened with your dad. That must be hard."

"Yeah, it is," Josh replied as he was confused about how to respond to Tad.

"Sorry for being a real jerk to you. I shouldn't have done that. And you have some pretty cool friends that take up for you." Tad said.

Josh looked over at the group and said, "Yeah, they are pretty cool."

Tad said, "Everyone thinks that I have friends like this, but the reality is that I don't."

Josh could see Tad's vulnerability, "Hey, listen when all this is done, hang out with us anytime."

"Thanks, Josh, I would like that," Tad said.

The sound of tires burning out from turning curves could be heard outside. The group knew that Barry was coming.

"Do you want to come with us?" Josh asked Tad.

"I think I will sit this one out but let me know if you need anything when you get back," Tad said.

"Thanks again!" Josh said as the group began to go outside.

Chapter 6

Finding Help

Barry's van pulled up to a sudden stop in front of Tad's house. Loud heavy metal music was playing from the van that could be heard all over the neighborhood. The group ran and got in the black van with flames down the side, saying, "Chariot of Fire" on the side and slid the door shut. Barry's van and life were more about the experience than it was about travel. Bub often said that he should have been born in the '90s. There were clothes all stashed throughout the back. Nowhere to really sit except for the front two seats. As he took off, he looked at Bub sitting in the passenger seat, "All right, little dudes, where are we going?"

"First, no filming, Barry," Bub said.

"What! Are you serious?" Barry replied back, "This is quality footage stuff for 'Adventures with Barry', have you seen what all is happening around here?"

"Barry!" Bub said defiantly.

"Ok," Barry dropped his head a little, "So where are we going?"

"Point Arena Lighthouse," Yashi said.

Barry slammed on the brakes. "Wait a second. You want me to leave Valley Hills?"

"Yes, Barry, we have to go to Point Arena in the next town over," Bub replied with almost a sarcastic tone.

"Dudes, do you understand how much Valley Hills is on lockdown?" Barry continued, "They are searching for these two dudes that were apparently going to unleash the robots on everyone and start to kill everyone in Valley Hills. Then these two guys are nowhere to be found. Then they go looking for his kid, and he isn't there. So, everyone is in like search mode around Valley Hills. Luckily Dek Bale was able to stop it before it all unleashed. So, who are your friends here?" As he began to drive some more.

Bub looked at Barry and said, "Barry, you aren't hearing the complete story. And these are my friends, Yashi, Terra, and Josh Nunley."

Barry slammed on the brakes again. "Nunley, like you any relationship to Cal Nunley?"

"Yeah, he's my dad," Josh replied, not knowing what Barry would do next.

Barry looked at Bub and said, "You mean to tell me that I have a fugitive in my van. You mean to tell me that I am aiding a fugitive right now in my van. Bub, you are going to get me in so much trouble with mom and dad."

Bub realized at this moment that Barry wasn't thinking about the legal side of things, and so he replied to Barry, "Hey, I won't say anything to them if you won't."

Barry said, "You promise?"

Bub said, "Yeah, man, you're my brother."

Then almost unaware of the consequences, Barry said, "Cool, I have never aided a fugitive before."

Josh said, "Well, technically, I'm not the fugitive, my dad is."

"But that's your family, and you guys are connected, so yeah, I'm helping you out, bro!" Barry replied, almost considering more of the street credit he would get with his fellow employees.

Barry continued, "Just know right now the police have the exit to Valley Hills covered up with roadblocks. They have dogs and scanners and stuff, not sure how we can get you out."

Terra then spoke up, "What about Old River Rd off of Outer Hills Rd? My dad used to tell me there was a road that no one really knows about that leads you out of Valley Hills, but not many people know about it for some reason."

Everyone else looked at each other and said, "Ok, let's go for it."

Barry took off towards Outer Hills. As they were driving around a corner, they passed the sign that read Bender's Curve. Josh screamed out, "Wait! Stop the van!"

Barry pulled off of the side. Josh immediately jumped out. No one knew what he was doing. They then jumped out as well to follow Josh. He ran to the sign for Bender's Curve and stopped and just stared out in the distance. The others soon caught up with Josh and were out of breath.

"Josh, what is wrong?" Yashi asked.

"Man, you can't just jump out like that!" Terra said.

"Guys, maybe he needs to go to the restroom," Bub said.

"It was here," Josh said. "It was down this road that my mom died, and I was born. Twelve years ago, today. Somehow, I believe this is all connected to this. Why come by this road tonight with all this happening?"

"Dude, that is deep?" Barry pierced the silence. "Barry, shut up!" Bub said.

"Guys, we have to find my dad. We have to find out what happened." Josh said.

As they slowly began to walk back to the van, they realized the magnitude of what was in front of them.

Barry slowly turned down Old River Rd. There were many old trees, and their limbs seemed to bend perfectly over the road. The path looked as if a vehicle had recently come down the path, but not enough to make a lasting impression on the road. As they drove along, the night seemed to get darker. There was a sign that read, "Bridge Ahead." When they pulled up to the bridge, they noticed that it was run down. Barry stopped the van and left the lights on. He got out and looked at the bridge and came back to the group and said, "Well, dudes, slight problem."

"What do you mean, a slight problem?" Bub asked.

Barry replied, "There is a piece of the bridge that is missing, and I am not sure if I can make it over to the other side without getting stuck. The only hope that we have is if I drive along the edge and then drive perfectly across this one board that is there."

Bub asked, "So what's the problem?"

Barry said, "Well, if I slip off the board, then we will more than likely be stuck, or we will fall in. And I'm not sure if I want to lose the chariot of fire." This was the name of his van.

Bub looked at Barry and said, "Do you want to be the dweeb that almost crossed a bridge, or do you want to be the guy that said, what bridge and crossed it anyway?"

Barry looking almost inspired by Bub's words, "Little bro dude, I love you, man." Barry then slammed on the gas pedal, and the van started speeding towards the part in the bridge. And as everyone started to scream and not look at the outcome. Barry sped across the bridge and slammed on the brakes on the other side. Everyone jumped out and looked back at the bridge at the amazement of how they just survived.

Barry got out and yelled in excitement, "Wasn't that awesome! Did you see that?"

Bub finally realized they were safe and reached over and hit Barry as hard as he could on the arm while he said, "Don't you ever do that again! Someone else sit up here in the front."

Josh jumped into the front seat as they slowly continued to drive down the road and eventually turned on the highway leading towards Point Arena.

As they drove along, Barry asked Josh, "So why to Point Arena Lighthouse?"

My dad told me to find my Aunt Abby, and this is the last picture that we have of where she was. I thought it was at least worth a start.

"Cool dude, finding and protecting family and stuff." Barry continued, "You have to have family, and you have to love them, even when they are unlovable. Do you know why I would do anything for Bub back there? It's because we are family. Have I hurt him? You bet! Have I done some crazy things? You bet! But I still love the little dude."

Josh said, "I have never thought about it like that before."

"Yeah man, through thick or thin, you stay with your family," Barry said.

Chapter 7

A Link is Found

The van pulled slowly into Point Arena Lighthouse. The only light was that coming from the lighthouse on top. It was late, and it seemed a storm was coming in. Yet in the lighthouse museum, there was a faint candle shining in a window.

"Looks like nobody is home," Barry said.

"Do you just go up to the door and knock on it?" Yashi asked.

"And what do I say?" Josh replied. "Hi, there was someone who took a picture here not too long ago, do you think there's a chance they are still around?"

It started to rain, and then all of a sudden, two sets of headlights appeared from off in the distance coming to where the van was located. Yashi hollered out, "Someone is coming! Come on, let's go!" They all jumped back into the van, and Barry began to try and speed off. However, as the headlights got closer, Barry was on a road he had never been down. As he turned a corner to try and getaway, the van began to spin out on the road and eventually stopped with one set of the tires in a ditch. There was nowhere that the group could go. Then both of the vehicles pulled up right beside the van shining spotlights on the van.

They ran up to the van, threw open the door, and one of the men had an African accent and spoke forcefully, "What are you doing here at this time of night? We should call the police."

Barry began to speak in an octave higher in his voice, "Don't shoot or kill us? I am merely the driver. They are the ones that you want."

The man again spoke up, "What are your names?"

In a total state of horror, they each began to give their full names: Terra Smith, Yashi Kasai, Josh Nunley, Buford Ulysses Brown.

The name caught everyone off guard. Yashi even said out loud, "Buford Ulysses…"

Bub replied, "it's a family name."

"QUIET," the man said. Then looking at Josh, he said, "Did you say, Josh Nunley?"

Thinking that he may have been with ProTech or Valley Hills, he nodded, not knowing what would happen next.

The man got on his walkie-talkie and said, "I have the Nunley boy."

All of a sudden, a woman's voice came through on the other side, "Josh?"

"Yes, Josh," The man replied.

"Bring him here immediately." The woman's voice said.

"What about the others?" The man asked.

"Others? I guess you bring them too." The woman replied.

"Ok, let's all go. Josh, Terra, and Yashi ride with me. The rest of you will ride in the other vehicle."

Barry spoke up, "Wait a second! You expect me to just leave my van out here for anyone to come and get."

The man looked sternly at Barry and said, "Yes, I do! Now get in the vehicle."

"Ok," Barry replied quickly, understanding he was not in a place to negotiate.

As the vehicles drove off, Josh looked at the man and asked him, "Are you with ProTech?"

"No, sir. We are not!" The man replied.

"Are you with Valley Hills?" Josh asked.

"No, we are not." The man said.

"CIA or FBI?" Yashi asked.

"Ha-ha, you ask a lot of questions, which is good. But no, we are not."

"So, who are you guys? Terra asked.

"We are the Protectors." The man said. My name is Tagufi from Zimbabwe, but the Protectors call me Thomas."

"Thomas, who were you talking to?"

"I can't tell you that yet, it's a surprise," Thomas replied. "How did you escape from Valley Hills?"

"How did you know people are looking for me?" Josh asked.

"Your father is all over the news. We wondered if you would come." Thomas said. "I told the others that I believed you could get here." At that moment, Thomas pulled beside the lighthouse. "Ok, we are here."

"Here? There was no one here," Yashi asked.

"Come on, I will show you," Thomas said.

They got out and then could hear as the other vehicle shut off, Barry and Bub arguing over something in the back seat. The driver got out, rolled their eyes, and looked at Thomas and said, "Brothers…"

They walked into the bottom of the lighthouse. Josh asked, "so are we going to the top?"

Thomas replied, "No, actually, we are going to the bottom." He slid the bottom of a light fixture that opened up a secret door that led down into a dark hole. He got out his flashlight and said, "Follow me," as he took off down the hole.

Slowly each one began to follow the other down the hole. They were walking down a set of winding stairs, almost opposite of the lighthouse stairs. They could hear some talking back and forth when they came down, almost arguing. Josh could vaguely pick up the last words, "he is our best hope. Now let me talk with him."

He noticed a tall woman standing at a table with others surrounding it. He also noticed there was what looked to be benches set up around a podium in a corner. A couple of small desks had computers hooked up to them with many wires coming out of them. Then there was a small desk that looked like a radio system used during old wars that Josh had seen in history books.

"Josh, I am so glad you made it. You must have gotten your father's message." The woman said.

"Aunt Abby?" Josh replied.

"Yes, I'm Aunt Abby," as she ran over and gave him a big embrace. "And I believe it is your birthday, correct?" Abby replied.

"Yes, mam, it is," Josh replied.

"What a way to spend a birthday, right?" Abby said. "I see that you have been talking a little with my friend Thomas."

"What are we doing here?" Josh asked.

Abby started to bring Josh and the group over to an older looking computer. "Josh, let me show you something that I believe will help." She then clicked on an icon folder named "Deborah." All of a sudden, he saw his mother's face come up on the screen. She clicked play, and it was her speaking:

Abby,

I just left Dek Bale's office, and I noticed that he was doing something unethical with Noah. He was trying to make it into a killer. He made a threat against my life. I believe that I may know too much. I am not sure if Dek knows about what is called Protector mode that I secretly put on Noah. I am about to be here to see Cal. Please do not say anything to him for his protection. But you can maybe do something to help. Check with a former employee of ProTech named Thomas, and he can help. Please keep sharing the truth.

As the video faded out, she was grasping her cross necklace, and Josh realized he was doing the same thing as he was touching the screen.

Abby looked at Josh and said, "This video that I received on that night began something that we have been working on for twelve years. And when I found out that your mother passed away, I knew that this video was even more of a key to what she was talking about that night. Your dad mentioned how, on that night, the car went into an unexplainable driving mode and started to speed around Bender's

Curve like never before. I believe that it wasn't a glitch on that night but that your parents were being targeted for what they knew that could bring down ProTech and all of Valley Hills."

Josh replied, "You also mean to take down Dek Bale?"

Abby looked at Thomas, "I told you he was a bright young man." She then looked at Josh and continued, "You are right! We believe that in the middle of all these events is Dek Bale. And we believe that we have a responsibility to protect the truth that has been taken away from the people of Valley Hills."

"Is that why Thomas called you The Protectors?" Josh asked.

"Yes! Did your father ever tell you why I never visit you in Valley Hills?" Abby asked.

"He said that you didn't like the city life and that your job was about being a teacher far away," Josh said.

Abby said, "Well, that is partly true. I don't like the city. But the reality is that at one time, I did live in Valley Hills. I moved there not long after your father and mother moved there. I had a flower shop, and my husband was a pastor."

"A pastor? Like of the Valley Hills church." Josh asked.

Abby replied, "Well, he was a pastor of a church there in the city, and we didn't practice all the other religions. Instead, we only read and lived by what the Bible said. When Dek Bale came and heard him speak one time, it was shortly after that that he required anyone to live in Valley Hills that was to be a part of a church had to be a part of the Valley Hills church. This meant that you couldn't read only the Bible, but you had to read other religious writings. My husband, Ty, rather than caving, decided that it was time for our church to begin to meet in secret. We would often meet in our home, but when that became too hard to do because of our neighbors, we began to meet at our business and called them "Flower workshops." But we realized that we were called to protect the truth and share the truth. Unfortunately, one night, our church was discovered because of what we believe was an infiltrator. And Ty was taken away, and I haven't seen him since. Your mother was a part of our church. Our symbol was the cross necklace, and we always had roses in our house."

Josh remembered at that moment the rose that sat next to the pictures on the dresser in the No-Go room. Abby continued, "And after Ty was captured, I realized that they would soon come after me. So rather than sitting around, the best thing for me to do was to escape. Then after your mother's message, I was able to find Thomas, and he helped me to build this place for others that want to protect the truth. And now this has all come about, and we are at the perfect time to expose Dek Bale and find Ty."

"Find Ty?" Josh asked.

"Yes, I believe that Ty is still living. Thomas was put into prison for being a pastor as well. Deborah knew this, and that is why she encouraged me to find him." Abby said.

"Yes, I knew Ty, but I also knew your mother as I worked at ProTech in the security division. When I saw some of the things that were happening with Bale and Broderick, I knew that my time would soon be over there." Thomas said, "But the one thing that I knew, is that God had a plan for me, He always has, and He always will. And my plan and purpose became to protect the message of the way."

"The way?" Bub asked.

"Yes, before computers, before Protech and Valley Hills, there was a way of life that was unlike all others. It was a way to live that was different from the world. It was a way that follows the way of Jesus. So, we seek to show sacrifice, love, community, and growth, just as Jesus did."

"Jesus?" Josh asked, "I have heard of him before in my church, isn't he just one of the ways to be in heaven. Didn't he just live and die?"

"That is where ProTech messed everything else up." Abby said, "Jesus isn't just a 'way,' He is THE Way. And yes, he did die, but he didn't stay that way, a miracle happened when He arose again. But not everyone believes this, and they have tried to tell people lies about The Way. That is why we are called The Protectors that are trying to protect the message of truth about who Jesus really is and make sure others hear about his death and his resurrection."

Josh looked around the room and noticed how everyone was staring at him and Abby. "Every person here, Josh, has lost family, their jobs, money, positions, but following Jesus and being a Protector is worth it." Abby said, "And every person will have to decide, is following The Way worth it?"

Thomas then spoke up, "He is worth it." Other men and women around the room all stood and said, "He is worth it!"

Josh was overwhelmed with the powerful, emotional moment. He could see how everyone was inspired to take action, so he asked, "So what do we do about ProTech? They have Noah, Ty, and we have to find my father."

Abby's face lit up, and she said, "That's right! Here is what we know. The update was an apparent glitch for Bale and ProTech."

Thomas chimed in, "Yes, but we believe that the glitch was a way to frame your father and James Newton."

Barry then asked, "But how can we prove it?"

"Noah is the key." Abby said, "If we can get to Noah, then we can show the Protector mode, and that is a start to reveal the plan."

"What is the Protector mode?" Terra asked.

"It was a secret code put onto only Noah by Deborah. It was meant to be a reversal of reverse zombie destructive mode. If we can show that the code was enacted, it will prove that Bale was behind the glitch, since your father didn't know the code." Abby said.

"When we get Noah, we get the code," Thomas said.

Suddenly, there was an alarm that began to go off. Abby looked at the computer on her desk, "Perimeter alarm! Does anyone else know where you are?"

"No mam," Josh replied.

"Thomas, go check it out," Abby ordered.

Thomas immediately took off. Abby said, "Ok, everyone to the bunker room." She motioned towards a wall, and there seemed to be only a map on the wall of Northern California. She pulled the map up, and it revealed a metal door built into the wall. She pushed forward the door and immediately shuffled the group into the room. As they huddled in the room, they could hear a different commotion outside. A few moments later, everything became really quiet. They sat in silence, waiting for what would happen next. Suddenly they heard the door beginning to open. The group moved back from the doors, not knowing what would happen next?

Abby then threw open the door, "Josh, come here."

Josh reluctantly moved forward. When he stepped out, he saw James Newton, dirty, wet, and exhausted sitting in a chair. Abby was questioning James intensely.

"Why did you come here?" Abby asked.

"Cal told me to come. He said that you could protect me." James said, "It's all a setup. Cal was set up, and I have proof."

"What kind of proof do you have?" Thomas asked.

"Well, I don't have the proof, but I know there is proof that exists." James said, "We ran a trace of the codes to have evidence how Cal didn't put it in. And when I realized that there was no way that Cal could have put in the code, I tried to tell Jezzie. But when I saw that Jezzie was called away to be questioned by Bale, I thought the only thing for me to do was to escape." Abby looked back at Thomas and asked, "The same Jezzie?" Thomas nodded.

James continued, "So I ran away, and when I got to my car, Cal was hiding in the back seat. He told me about Abby and helped me to send the message to you through Noah. Cal realized that all of Valley Hills was going to be looking for him. So, he had me drop him off at the old flower shop downtown. I took Old River Rd, and I was able to escape by the old bridge."

James looked at Josh and said, "When I saw the news again, I saw that they had captured your father at the flower shop. Bale has him, and I am not sure what they are going to do with him."

"How can we trust you? How do we know that you aren't leading Bale to us now?" Abby asked.

"I am not, trust me! If I were leading Bale to you, he would be here with me. I have told you all I know, and I don't know of anyone else to go to for help. We have to stop Bale and ProTech."

Josh looked at Abby and pleaded, "We have to get my father back!"

Abby stood in a commandeering position, "Everyone, this is our time. This is the Protector's time. We have to go and rescue Noah, Cal, and Ty! It will be dangerous, but we have to go! Are you all ready? Josh, you guys can stay here with James and be protected."

"Wait! No!" Josh exclaimed, "I have to go after my father! I have to go after Noah!"

"It's just too dangerous, and I will not lose another family member." Abby said, "Thomas prepare the others. James, you can stay here and recover as well. If there is anything that we need, you can hear us through the radio. We will maintain contact."

Josh was disappointed along with the others, but Abby was defiant in her position as she said, "It's time to go Protectors."

Chapter 8

Hacking the Firewall

Abby left some drinks and snacks for the group. Bub and Barry were the first to run over to the table to begin feeding their starving appetites. Yashi and Terra had gotten some snacks and turned back to see Josh sitting by the radio. "What is he doing?" Yashi asked Terra. "I'm not sure," Terra said as she grabbed an extra drink and snack and walked over to where Josh was sitting.

She tapped him on the shoulder with the drink. Josh barely turned his head and replied, "I'm not interested. Someone has to be here in case something goes wrong."

"Josh, you have to eat and drink, and they just left, so we have some time." Terra tried to reason with Josh as she held up the can again beside his shoulder. He reluctantly reached back and took the drink and snacks from her hand.

"Why did you want to go so bad?" Terra asked.

"I just feel like I need to be there to help," Josh replied.

"But what can we really do. There could be guns and stuff there." Terra asked.

"Yeah, I know, but I want to know that I at least tried to save my dad and Noah," Josh said.

Suddenly, Josh felt the presence of someone overlooking his shoulders. He looked up, and it was James Newton. "May I join you?"

"Yes, sir, by all means," Josh replied.

"Josh, can I tell you something?" James asked.

"Sure," Josh said.

"Your father thinks the world of you. I think you are the bravest guy I know. I mean, when I heard about your family's courage, I can see so much of them in you." James said.

"Thank you, Mr. Newton," Josh replied. "And he wanted me to make sure that I told you…"

All of a sudden, there were some sounds coming through the radio. It was Abby and the team. Josh realized that he was only able to hear all the team's communication among one another and not speak back to them since there was not a microphone. It sounded like the team divided between two groups. One team was with Thomas, and the other was with Abby. Thomas' team was going for the prison to try and free Cal and Ty, while Abby's team went for the Alpha Team's office to retrieve Noah and the trace code.

Josh could hear how the teams used a large underground sewage system to get into Valley Hills undetected. Thomas came over the radio.

"Abby Team, Abby Team, come in." Thomas' voice could be overheard.

"This is Abby Team, copy." Abby's voice came through clear.

"Abby Team, let me know when you get into position, and we will begin to coordinate," Thomas said.

"10-4!" Abby said. The group was hanging on every sound.

About 2 minutes of radio silence passed while Josh and the others waited patiently to listen for anything new. Then Abby's team began to come through with a whisper, "Thomas Team, Thomas Team, this is Abby Team, do you copy?"

"Go ahead Abby Team," Thomas replied.

"We are in position, ready to enter the building," Abby said.

"10-4, Abby Team, we are in position as well," Thomas said.

Abby then came back on whispering, "Remember when we get to the offices you need to…wait, wait, wait! What do you mean, what are we doing here?"

Something was wrong, and Josh could tell that Abby started to speak to someone she was standing beside. "We are just waiting here to see some friends. This is just a radio that I carry with me." Josh could tell Abby was secretly pushing the button on her radio to let everyone know what was going on to her and the team. Suddenly the radio went silent, and Josh started to get confused about how they got caught. He looked at the others and said, "We have to do something."

"But what can we do?" Yashi asked.

"We have to go and help them!" Josh said.

"Yeah, but how?" Terra asked.

"Chariot of Fire," Josh said.

Barry's perked up, "Yes! Yes! It's time for the Chariot of Fire!"

James Newton was confused and asked, "What is the Chariot of Fire?"

A few minutes later, the group was at the van with Barry saying to James, "This is the Chariot of Fire!"

Bub said, "Check it out, it's stopped raining. Maybe ole Jesus is going to help us out on this one."

"Let's load up big and little dudes," Barry said.

They were able to pull off immediately, Barry turned up the music a little louder as they drove off and started to head back to Valley Hills. James Newton asked, "So what is our plan?"

Josh said, "We have to get to the main office. Once we get there, then we will be able to find out what happened to Abby and her team. We are going to have to try to get in through the sewers just like what they did."

Barry then shouted to the group, "Don't worry, I know a shortcut." And with a quick turn of the wheel, they turned off onto a dirt road. "Yeah, I once dated a girl that liked to come to the sewers, always thought she was kind of cool until that is the only place she wanted to hang out in."

"You dated a girl that liked the sewers?" Bub asked.

"Hey, don't talk about Jeanine like that!" Barry replied to Bub as if they were in a brother-to-brother squabble about Barry's dating life.

About five minutes later, they pulled up to a large tunnel. "There it is," Barry said.

Josh looked at the group and said, "Hey, I am not sure what is going to happen here, and if you don't want to go, I completely understand."

Yashi then spoke up, "Hey Josh; this is our time to be Protectors too! I say, let's go."

Josh replied, "Ok, let's do it."

When they got to the tunnel, the smell was bad, realizing what they were going to have to walk through not to be seen entering Valley Hills. Luckily Barry had walked through the tunnels before with Jeanine and had come out close to one of the entrances to ProTech.

Before they went up, Josh said, "We need a diversion, so ProTech security won't be looking for us. Does anyone have any ideas?"

Everyone stood around and tried to think for a little bit.

Terra then spoke up, "I have an idea, but it will take a phone call."

"Let's go for it!" Josh said.

Terra then stepped away from the group and started to make a phone call. The group could overhear her, saying, "Yes, I need it done right now and grab as many people as possible to help or else."

She then stepped back to the group and said, "He said that we should be able to know when the coast is clear."

"He?" Bub asked, "Who is he?"

"I don't want to say," Terra replied.

The group began to banter back and forth with Terra until it finally reached a point of her saying, "It's Tad, okay! I called and asked for Tad's help."

"Oh ok," The group at first was silent after her response.

"Tad? Really, Tad?" Bub asked.

The group again began to banter back and forth, making kissing sounds about Tad and Terra.

"Do you want me to show you how I motivated Tad?" Terra began to ask everyone in the group with a fist held up to their faces.

"No, you win!" Josh replied as the group conversation about Terra and Tad died down.

A few minutes had passed when there was what sounded like something being rolled over the manhole cover. Josh and Bub thought it best to look out the top together.

Josh and Bub slowly began to lift the manhole cover to see what was happening above them and to look for the diversion. They could see some guards that were standing by one of the doors talking to each other. When they looked their way, they tried to lower the manhole cover as silently as they could.

"What's going on? Yashi asked.

"Nothing yet!" Bub replied. As they were about to lower back down, Bub said, "Look, Josh!" At that time, a couple of kids on bikes cycled by the entrance. Then there were a couple of more from a different direction. Before long, there were what seemed like kids coming from every direction. The guards by the doors at first were like, "Hey, you guys get out of here!" Trying to use only their words. But then all of a sudden, one of the kids that came cycling by started to throw what looked like fireworks at the guards. Then before long, each pair of riders came by and threw them.

Finally, one of the guards began to say, "we are going to need some help here at the front entrance." Then he looked at the other guard and said, "Ok, let's get them," as they started to run away from the building. Before long, more guards started to come out to run out away from the front door. Then in Bub-like fashion, there was the sound of an eagle that started to be made. Bub looked at Josh and said, "That's the sign. Let's go!"

Bub and Josh lifted the cover to see the guards trying to chase the different kids on bicycles away from the entrance. The rest of the team ran into the front door and made their way to the stairwell to be out of sight.

Josh stopped the group and said, "We need to split up. Yashi, James, and I will go to the office upstairs. And Bub, Barry, and Terra, you try to go to the prison and find Thomas' team."

"Where is the prison located?" Terra asked.

James spoke up and said, "If you go down two levels, you will find a hallway corridor that connects from ProTech's storage to the police building. It will be guarded."

"Great," Bub said sarcastically, "Send us right to the guards and prison."

James responded, "You will go past the kitchen."

"Ok, let's go!" Bub replied immediately, and with that, the group began to take off.

Barry stopped Josh before they split and handed him his lenses, "Dude, if you get any footage, please stream it! Like shooting or sneaking around, please get it, my cred would immediately go up on Spot-On."

Yashi, James and Josh, took off up the stairs. James said to Josh, "We have to find a way to hide ourselves; they will soon be coming down the stairs." About that time, a couple of guards in what sounded a couple of levels above stepped into the stairwell. One of them said to the other, "Come on, we have to get to the front door" and started down the steps towards Josh, Yashi, and James.

They were by one of the floor entrances and quickly looked down the hallway to make sure no one was coming and snuck over to the closest bathroom by the stairs and elevator. When the guards came running by, one of them stopped and said, "Hey, go on ahead, I want to check something!" as he noticed that the door was closing for no reason. He looked down the hall and at, first, didn't see anything. Yashi, Josh, and James were standing inside the men's bathroom on the toilet seats, so that thought if they looked in there, no one would see their feet. But as the guard walked down the hall, suddenly Yashi's foot slipped and splashed in the water, causing him to let out a whispered "Yuck!" The guard turned immediately and went back to the bathroom. He opened the door to not seeing any feet and decided to walk down to the furthest stall to begin to check. He went to the last stall, furthest away from the door. It was the one where Yashi was. He, all of a sudden, kicked open the door, where Yashi said in a foreign accent, "Is dis how you use the bathroom?" as he stood on the toilet seat.

"Get down!" the guard said as he turned around to take Yashi out of the stall. James hit him over the back of his head with a mop handle. It knocked the guard down to his knees. James then reached back again and hit him across the face with his fist, knocking the guard down the floor. Josh reached down and checked how the guard was merely knocked out. Yashi said, "Come on; let's get out of here." Josh said,

"Wait!" and he reached down and grabbed the keys, fabs, and radio from the guard. He then told James to pull off the guards' shirt and hat and put them on. James then took the guards handcuffs and cuffed his hands to the toilet pipes, then they took his belt and wrapped them around his feet and pulled one of his socks off and put it in his mouth to prevent him from screaming.

Josh, James, and Yashi came up with the idea at that moment to make it look like Josh and Yashi were caught outside by James looking like a guard, so they could take the elevator to the floor they needed. When they opened the bathroom door, they looked down the hall to check if anyone was coming. Luckily no one was there. James motioned for them to come out with him, and they went to the elevator.

They opened the elevator, and when they got in, they tried to select the floor for the Alpha Team. However, the floor was limited by only certain members of the security team or the Alpha Team, and the guard didn't have access to the floor. James hit the floor that was the highest they could go to with the guard's fab, which was the floor below. He then began to think of how he could get up to that floor. When the doors opened to the floor, there were some guards that were walking by. They nodded at James, thinking he was a fellow guard. James nodded back reluctantly and then moved out of the elevator to the hallway. He looked both ways as if he was lost. The reality is that James had never been on this floor that looked like the main security floor, as guards were walking around everywhere. The structure of the floors was generally the same, so James thought that he could get them to one of the offices that were around the walls of the floors. He just had to try and get them to the right one. Suddenly, one of the guards walked by and said, "Hey, take any kids you find to one of the examination rooms this way," as the guard pointed down the hallway.

"Yes, sir!" James replied like the best guard he could be. He then walked into the area and noticed an empty office to the right. He pulled the boys to the office and got out his phone. He looked at Josh and said, "The only person that I think I can call is Jezzie. He would be able to help us and would keep it a secret. He tried to help us before."

"Is this the same Jezzie that Abby and Thomas mentioned?" Josh asked.

"Yeah, I'm not sure why they did, but it's the only plan that I can come up with," James said. He grabbed his phone and called Jezzie.

"Jezzie. Jezzie, It's James. What is that loud music in the background? I am here in ProTech on the 9th floor in an office. Don't worry about how I got here. I have Cal's son with me. We need to get on the Alpha Team floor. Can you help us?" James asked. "Great thanks, see you in a moment."

When they hung up, he looked at Yashi and Josh and said that he was here in the building, and he was coming to get us. About that moment, a guard walked in the office, and began questioning James, "What are you doing in here? Who are these kids? Why are they here?"

"Sorry sir, I thought this was one of the investigation rooms!" James replied. "These are kids that are causing problems outside that I caught."

"Who is your supervisor?" the guard asked.

"Uhh, uhh." James began to stutter.

Suddenly, Jezzie busted into the room and said, "There you are! Thank you for bringing them all here. Broderick wants to meet the guard that brought in these boys. Let's go!"

Jezzie began to shuffle the boys and James out of the room towards the elevators. He looked back at the guard that was questioning James and said, "Great work, sir! Bale will be very happy with your work."

"Thank you," as the guard was seemingly confused about what just happened.

Bub, Barry, and Terra made their way down the stairs to the second lower level. They slowly opened the door to an empty hallway. They slowly slipped out into the hall and began to make their way towards the kitchen. When they got there, they noticed how there was a door that led to the storage area, but it was locked. Suddenly, they could hear a radio going off nearby. It was a guard that was on patrol. The group decided to hide in the kitchen in different places. Barry and Terra dashed to hide at the end of a counter on the floor. Bub was trying to slide his body in a small nook beside the refrigerator. He was able to get some of his body back there, but when the guard entered, he had to stop struggling to be quiet.

The guard was walking around the kitchen and even went over to a small cabinet, where he had a secret stash of food. He began to eat his food looking around, when all of a sudden, he noticed the small foot sticking out from the side of the refrigerator. He began to walk down the counter towards where Bub was trying to hide. He was almost about to reach around and grab Bub when all of a sudden, Barry jumped up and made the crane move from Karate Kid to get the guard's attention. "Hey!" The guard said. Suddenly, the refrigerator door whipped open and knocked the guard to the floor. Terra then grabbed a pan and knocked the guard over the head to knock him out. They grabbed his keys and fabs and began to getaway. Bub struggled to get out from behind the refrigerator while Barry stood there and watched him and said, "Dude, you have to get off the twinkies!"

"Shut up, Barry," Bub replied, "What move was that?"

Barry tried to make his best impression from the movie, "One day I teach you about wax on and wax off."

Terra then said, "Come on, guys, we have to go!"

They were able to open the door with the guard's keys and head down the corridor. The hallway was lined with large pipes with large enough spaces between them that made it an easy place for them to slip into and hide. The hallway was completely dark except for the light coming from a small window on a door at the end of the hallway.

They slowly began to approach the door. They noticed that there were guards posted on the other side and not on the side that Bub, Barry, and Terra approached. They could start to hear the guard was waking up and hollering. Barry told the others to hide with the keys. He then walked up to the door and tapped on the glass. The guards were shocked as they turned around to see someone on the other side that was not with ProTech. They immediately opened the door, and Barry took off running. The guards were chasing him, and before the door closed back, Terra and Bub were able to slip inside the doors.

When Barry ran back through the kitchen, the guard was still recovering by the door that opened to the storage area. Barry did some sort of a football, ballet spin move to avoid getting captured by the guard, and about that time, the door swung open, and the other two guards ran into the other guard already in the kitchen, sending all three of them to the floor. Barry looked back while he ran and said, "Adventures with Barry is missing so much good footage!"

When Bub and Terra entered the hallway, they noticed that there were in prison, and different people were sitting in the cells. Suddenly, they noticed Thomas sitting there in a cell. He had been beaten some. "Thomas, Thomas," Terra whispered. "Its' us...Terra and Bub."

Thomas looked up and cracked a smile. "Protectors, yes!" About that time, a guard entered the area and said, "Hey, how did you get down here?" He walked down to where Bub and Terra were, and he held up a taser to them. Bub and Terra moved against the cells opposite of Thomas' and stood there at first with their arms up. Then the guard got a call on his radio that lowered his taser for a moment, Bub then let out a war cry and bull-rushed the guard that pushed him against the cell. Thomas was able to reach through and grab the guard while Terra grabbed his fab that opened the prison cell door. Thomas and Bub were able to push him into the cell and tie him up at that moment. Once Thomas took control of the situation, Bub sat down for a moment like he had run a race, "I need a snack." Then realizing what all happened, he stood up and did a little victory dance for showing his courage.

Thomas grabbed the fab, keys, and radio of the guard and went down the hallway and began to unlock the doors. There were those that were a part of the Protectors team. Then there was a guy that they hadn't seen before. "Where is Cal?" Terra asked.

"We don't know!" Thomas said, "He must be with Bale. We have to get you guys out of here!"

"Out of here?" Terra asked. "We are the reason that you are out. Let's go and get them together!" Thomas couldn't deny the efforts of Terra and Bub. "Ok, but we have to get Ty out of here. He motioned to a couple that had been at the lighthouse and for them to help carry Ty out. They opened the door to the corridor, and all began to head back to ProTech. When they reached the kitchen storage, Bub and Terra motioned for everyone to be cautious. Thomas put his ear up to the door, then hearing that someone was coming, he motioned for everyone to hide along some of the piping along the walls. Suddenly, the three guards came rushing through the hallway heading back to the prison. While the guards entered the prison doors, Thomas and the others slipped through the other door. Once everyone was through the door, Thomas and the others pushed the kitchen counter in front of the door, realizing that they would soon try to come back.

The group then went up to the stairwell to go up to the main level. Right as they were about to head up the stairs, Barry came running out of a room. "Whew! I am glad to see you guys! I had to give them the shake and bake!" Barry boasted.

When they walked up to the main level, Thomas spoke up, "Ok, listen, Ty, we are getting you out of here to the sewers." And he motioned for the couple and others to begin to head out. After they left, Thomas then looked at Bub, Terra, and Barry, "Ok guys, you ready to be Protectors? Let's go!"

They then took off up the stairs.

As Jezzie, James, Josh, and Yashi entered the elevator, James looked at Jezzie and asked, "What are you doing here so late? I thought you would be out of here. Where is the trace code?"

Jezzie replied, "I have it with me here."

James was shocked at Jezzie's response and said, "You mean that you never got the code out of here. That is the only thing that will vindicate Cal and me. Why is it still here?" As he said that, the elevator doors chimed and began to open.

Jezzie's gaze and tone began to change, "James, there are some circumstances that have changed.

Chapter 9

The Crash

As the doors opened, it was not to the Alpha Team floor; instead, there was loud music blaring that James noticed was the same that Jezzie could hear. This was Bale's office floor that no one was allowed to see. After the encounter with Deborah, Bale moved his office quarters to this floor away from the Alpha Team. The room was overwhelming for its art and decorations. There was a wall of screens sitting in front of one chair. Then there was a door that had mirrored glass. The outer walls looked out over the city of Valley Hills in all directions.

From a set of couches, Bale stood up from sitting next to Zerah, he looked at Josh, James, and Yashi and started to clap his hands in sarcastic applause slowly. "Well, well, well, would you look at you guys! The world's greatest technological city ever created, still couldn't stop the infiltration of the Protectors."

Yashi whispered over to Josh, "How does he know about…"

Bale interrupted, "The Protectors, how do I know about the Protectors? Little man, everything that happens in this city I know about. In fact, everything that happens in this world, I am starting to know about. It is I who can keep an eye on things with Russia and China. I am able to control the world's leaders and economies. I am able to solve some of the world's greatest problems. And yet here we are tonight, with a problem that seems not to have a solution.

James spoke up, "Bale, these are children. Let them go! Whatever problem you think exists; we can discuss it between us."

Bale spoke up, "James, you don't understand that it's because of one of these children that my problems exist at ProTech. I have tried to go to the next level, to a place of total world domination all happening right here at ProTech, and yet this one family keeps being a thorn in my side. But not anymore, not tonight. Tonight, we make things right for ProTech!" About that time, a sound started to come from his desk. He simply moved his hand over the pad on his desk, and the voice of Broderick began to speak, "I have them here with me, sir."

"And what about the others? Were we able to get them back?" Bale asked.

"No, sir! We are still searching for them?" Broderick replied.

"I want this entire building and campus scoured. If they are not found, I am holding you personally responsible, Broderick." Bale said with a swipe of his hand in the opposite direction.

He continued, "Finding good help these days is hard. Thus, I am forced to do so much stuff on my own. Can I show you some of my latest work?"

He waved for them to come towards the mirrored door. "Come on!"

At first, they began to take a couple of steps back. However, Jezzie stopped their reluctance as he was standing there with a gun in his hand, and he started to move the gun in the direction for them to follow. James looked at Jezzie, "How could you?"

"As I told you, circumstances changed. It's time to follow Bale's directions." Jezzie replied.

As they walked through the door, they could see Cal and Abby sitting in chairs, with their mouths and hands bound, and Noah as well as in the room sitting down unaware of their presence.

Josh cried out, "Dad!" And he tried to run over to where they were sitting. But Jezzie stopped them from going.

Bale then spoke up, "Do you see how this is now a family affair? I can see the headline on Spot-On now, 'The Nunley Family; Valley Hills Greatest Criminals.' They would run you out of town. In fact, they would run you out of this world.

Josh then spoke up, "Bale, why? Why go through all of this?"

"Great question!" Bale said, "I guess that is the million-dollar question or let me restate that; I guess that is the 100 trillion-dollar question. I had perfectly positioned ProTech to become the exclusive provider of AL-Lis that could fight in battles. At first, there was reluctance having a military that was completely operated by computers and AL-Lis, and yet I needed to show that there were codes that could be implemented that could both start and stop an entire army with the click of a button. But I needed to convince the world that I had the control. So, I needed a…"

James then interrupted, "Glitch." As he began to put all the pieces together.

Bale replied, "That's right. In fact, what I really needed was someone to think that there was a glitch. So, I hired him for a couple of million dollars to put on someone else's code the reverse zombie code. Thus, enters Jezzie."

Everyone looked at Jezzie as he hung his head.

Jezzie spoke up, "He said he would take my family. I had no choice."

Bale then interrupted, "Wrong! We all have a choice. And we all have a price. Yours was just a lower price than others. So, we planned to set up Cal. But Jezzie knew how close you all were, so there was going to be the need to make sure that you were framed as well as James. Thus, we had you run the trace code." Bale pulled up the code and put it on the screen as he continued, "And whoever runs the trace code was going to be implicated for trying to erase the glitch. Thus, we had two pawns that we needed, really three," as Bale mocked Jezzie.

Yashi then spoke up, "But why come after Josh and Noah?"

Bale replied, "You see, there is a code that I needed from Noah. It was a code that I have been missing that I needed to extract from Noah to make sure that my plan can succeed. Josh was merely just a loose end in my plan."

"A loose end?" Josh replied. "Don't you mean that you wanted to kill me?"

"Killed is such a harsh word," Bale said with an air of superiority. "I much rather prefer the word, deprogrammed...forever. But now, I am about to extract the code from Noah. You showed up at just the right time. I was going to just do it for Cal and Abby, but now I can show the entire family, and you can all, oh, what did I just say, deprogram together...forever."

Bale then turned towards Noah and plugged a cord into his port and began to type on his computer. Josh looked around, trying to find some way to escape or stop Bale. He then noticed his father's eyes, and he had a look on his face as if he was trying to get Josh's attention. Cal used his eyes to encourage Josh to look down towards where his hands were tied behind his back. Josh looked down and noticed how there was a bottle of water sitting by his father's feet.

Josh spoke up, "You know I don't think that these AL-Lis work at all."

Bale then said, "Oh, really, a twelve-year-old boy is going to tell me about how to fix my life's work."

Josh said, "I am just saying that if I could overcome a Noah, then so will every other military. In fact, it makes your AL-Lis pretty lame. Who isn't to say that someone else won't come up with the solution, and then your 100 trillion-dollar plan becomes zero!"

Bale got angry and turned around and said, "Oh really, how about I turn on Noah right now just for fun to see how lame he is. I am about to de-program him right now; I just have to find that code."

Josh replied, "it's pretty sad that you have to get a robot to defeat a twelve-year-old boy."

Bale then got more frustrated and said, "Ok, that's it! Let's just take care of this now. He then clicked a couple of buttons, and Noah began to stand up." He then took out the port and clicked something on his phone and said, "Let's begin the deprogramming now with the Nunley's. How about we start with your father?"

Noah then turned to Cal and grabbed him and slung him across the room; when he landed, he was knocked out.

Bale then said, "You know what, let's go ahead and remove Aunt Abby as well."

Noah then grabbed her by the shoulders and picked her up and threw her across a table where she landed, writhing in pain.

Bale then said, "And for the finale, let's remove Josh, the Protector." And with a couple of clicks on the phone, Noah turned his attention towards Josh.

Josh then yelled out, "Now!"

James turned towards Jezzie and rushed him against the wall, trying to hold the gun away. There was a scuffle, and the gun came out of Jezzie's hands and slid across the floor. Yashi ran over to Bale and tried to bull rush him against the computer screens. Josh leaped towards the water bottle only to have his foot caught by Noah. As they pulled against each other, Josh was able to let his shoe slip off of his foot, grab the water bottle, and splash it on Noah. Noah stopped for a moment and stepped back, he shook his head again and started to advance violently towards Josh again, and Josh was able to hold up his fingers and yell to Noah, "Two of everything. Two of everything."

Everyone had stopped to see how Noah would respond. He stopped and looked at Josh's fingers just as he did before. Suddenly,

Noah picked up Josh, and Bale began to yell to Noah, "Finish him now!" Noah, then looked at Josh's fingers again and held his two fingers slowly up to Josh's and then said slowly, "Two of everything."

Bale noticed the gun at his feet, and he ran over and picked up the gun and, in a rage of fury, said, "Stop, everyone stop! I have had enough of this! It's time to end all of this!" He pointed the gun towards Josh and pulled the trigger. But at the last second, Noah jumped in front of the bullet, sending both him and Josh to the floor. Everyone was amazed at what just happened.

Suddenly, the glass from the mirrored door crashed through. It was the Valley Hills police. They were hollering, "Put the gun down! Put the gun down!" Bale immediately dropped the gun and said, "Arrest them! Arrest them all! I have caught all those responsible for the glitch."

The police then walked over to Bale. Then the chief walked in and said, "Mr. Bale, you are arrested! I believe you have some questions to answer to a lot of people."

"What?" Bale said in rage, "They are the ones that messed up! Not me! Arrest them!"

Then the police chief pulled out his phone and showed the live stream that was going on. "I got a tip from an old friend in security here that I needed to watch what was happening." As the chief looked back over his shoulder, Thomas was standing in the hall.

Bale looked at the screen and confused. He said, "Adventures with Barry, who is that?"

Barry then, with perfect timing busted in the room, "The most awesome show ever!" He was followed by Thomas, Bub, and Terra.

Josh stood up and took off his glasses and gave them to the police chief and said, "I believe everything you will need will be found here."

"Ok, guys, let's get him out of here." The police chief said. "And grab Jezzie too!"

"Wait!" James said. "Don't take him. He was being blackmailed into doing this."

"We will have to figure that out at the station." The chief said.

"I'll come and help you," James said to Jezzie.

"Thank you!" Jezzie replied as he hung his head.

Bale overwhelmed with rage, ran towards Josh and looked him in the eye, and said, "She can't protect you forever! I will find her and eliminate her!"

"Get him out of here! And find Broderick as well!" The chief said.

Josh was taken back with what he said, but then his attention was immediately turned towards the sparks that were flying from Noah on the floor. Josh could see that the bullet went through the center part of Noah's body, where the main hardware was stationed within Noah's frame. Josh put Noah's head in his lap, and he could realize that Noah's eyes were flashing, which was a sign that his power was waning.

Josh began to cry and look at Noah in his eyes, "Don't go! Don't go! Stay with me! We can fix you, Noah!" He looked up at everyone and said, "Someone help him! We have to help him!" Everyone was frozen as they realized how much damage had been done. Josh slowly started to realize the same thing.

He looked as tears ran down his face onto Noah's face and said, "You are my best friend. Thank you for always being there for me! I am sorry I couldn't protect you!"

Slowly Noah grabbed Josh's hand, and he positioned Josh's fingers into the number two signal. He put his fingers slowly connected to Josh's and said, "Two of everything." And then the light from his eyes dimmed. Josh looked at Noah and said, "Two of everything," and began to cry, rocking his body with his body as a mother rocks a child.

As the group left from ProTech's facilities, there was a crowd that had gathered after watching Barry's live stream to see what all happened. They could see Bale getting arrested. And then, slowly, the group: Abby, Thomas, Cal, James, Terra, Yashi, Bub, Barry, and Josh emerged from the building to thunderous applause. They were confused, and one of the police officers leaned over and said, "Someone said that for the first time, they feel free because of you guys!"

As Josh got into a vehicle to leave, he looked over and saw Tad standing there with many of his classmates on bicycles. He gave him a brief wave of appreciation. He then looked further in the distance, and Ellie Grace was standing there. She smiled and waved at Josh, where his heart sunk for a moment in disbelief that she was waving at him. They got into the cars and said, "Let's go to the lighthouse."

Chapter 10

The Miracle

When the group returned to the lighthouse, Bub and Barry's parents, along with Yashi and Terra's parents were all waiting on their arrival, which included a huge embrace by all of them. They each began to share their stories of what happened. Then as Aunt Abby walked in, she immediately noticed Ty sitting there. She ran up to him and gave him a huge hug and kiss. At first, he flinched as he was in pain, and she stopped for a moment, but then embraced him again as they began to cry with one another with joy. Cal and Josh walked in together, and Cal's arms were around Josh's shoulders. Josh had never experienced this type of embrace from his father. Yet the joy of being close to his dad overcame any awkwardness at that moment. Thomas walked in and spoke up, "Everyone, I am so excited to see the joy in this room! By God's grace and favor, we were able to see miracles today! You are all truly Protectors from this moment on! The best thing we can do is to give God all the glory!" With that, Thomas began to sing a song, "Praise God from whom all blessings flow..." Slowly other Protectors joined in singing, "Praise Him all creatures here below. Praise Him above ye heavenly host. Praise Father, Son, and Holy Ghost. Amen"

Abby then spoke up, "You know what this all calls for? A Celebration!"

Everyone cheered, and they began to gather up food and refreshments for everyone to enjoy a meal together. At the meal, everyone was laughing and celebrating. Bub and Barry seemed to continue to argue about food. Yashi and Terra were talking about some of their personal adventures. Josh looked around and noticed how the entire room was filled with joy. He then noticed how his father was sitting in the corner alone. Josh walked over to his father, "You not celebrating?"

Cal responded, "It's a bittersweet celebration, son. I love you so much, and I hate that I missed your life. I missed you so much. I am truly sorry for the father that I was. But I hope that you will forgive me and help me never to go back to be that kind of dad again."

Josh hugged his father, "Dad, I am so glad that I have you back!"

Aunt Abby came over and said to Josh and Cal, "Hey, do you want to see something cool?" She pulled out a drive and put it in a computer. "We were able to hack into Bale's computer and get some files. We have so much stuff that we are going to send to the police that is evidence against him. I am about to download it to the computer. I thought you would want to see how these files download and transfer."

"Cool!" Josh responded. He began to see how the files were all being transferred over to the computer. Their names began to flash across the screen. Suddenly, one caught his eye, and he yelled out, "Stop the download!" Abby stopped and said, "What is it?"

Josh said to Abby, "Scroll back up." Abby began to scroll. Cal leaned over and said, "Son, what is it?"

"Dad! Look!" as he motioned to the screen, there was a file named 'Deborah.'

Abby clicked on the file, and there were two video files titled, 'Deborah' and 'Deborah-final.' They were both dated on the day of her death. Josh clicked on the 'Deborah-final' file. When it opened, and they clicked play, it was from the hospital room. There were different sounds, and it looked like someone was filming a surgery being performed.

Cal then said, "Hey, wait. I remember this video. This is what Dek Bale showed me what happened to…"

Josh said, "What happened to whom?"

"To your mother," Cal said slowly.

As the group started to gather around, they could hear the video of the doctors and nurses.

"We have to make sure that the baby is taken care of."

"The baby is stable currently."

The sounds then began to blare on the video of alarms as someone called out. "She is crashing. She is crashing."

"Let's get the baby out."

The camera spanned the room, and suddenly, they could recognize that it was Deborah. Then there was the cry of a baby. It was from Josh. Then a team of doctors and nurses ran him out of the room.

"She's still crashing. She's still crashing."

Then the horrifying sound of the solid beep came through on the video, and the doctor was heard saying, "there is nothing more that can be done."

The video suddenly shut off.

The room quickly changed from a celebration to sadness at what they witnessed. Yashi and Terra came over to Josh. But Josh shook off their consolation. He couldn't believe what he just saw. Cal was sobbing!

Aunt Abby then said, "Josh, I am so sorry that you had to see that."

Josh then said, "It doesn't make sense."

Abby said, "What doesn't make sense?"

"What Bale said before he left," Josh said. "He looked at me and said that she can't protect me forever, and he will find her and eliminate her."

Bub spoke up, "He must have been talking about your Aunt Abby."

Josh said, "I just feel like there is something else."

He then looked at the other video and noticed how the one titled 'Deborah' was a little longer. His mind was racing. He said to himself, "what else could it be?"

Yashi said, "Are you sure that you want to watch it again?"

Josh said, "Yes, I am sure."

When the video came on, Josh noticed that it started in the same place. He skipped over to where the other video was about to end.

The video began to play.

"Let's get the baby out."

"She's still crashing. She's still crashing."

Then there was the beep heard, and the doctor said, "there is nothing more that can be done. Turn that video off."

The person taking the video began to struggle with finding the off button, and then a nurse yelled out, "Wait! Look!" And slowly, beeps began to pierce the room. Then someone said, "It's a miracle! Call Bale!"

Part 2. Restart

The reality is that life in Valley Hills was totally different since that night with Bale. After he was arrested, he convinced the police and mayor that Barry's video was a fake. He even bribed the mayor to declare an ordinance that made it illegal to post the video on any social media. Therefore, the people of Valley Hills began to believe in Bale's innocence. After he spent a brief time in jail, all charges were dropped by the City Prosecutor.

The damage to the company's image then became the primary concern. Bale agreed to step down as the CEO of ProTech to keep the company stable. Yet, he still was the primary stockholder of the company. Since then, he has not been seen in public. Rumors are that he is hiding somewhere within Valley Hills, while other rumors still remain of what really happened on that night. What has caused further confusion is that the city is currently experiencing random blackouts from the power grid and no one knows the cause.

When the video first went viral, the Northern California government chose to outlaw the use of ALLIs for personal use. Recently, ProTech, under the leadership of their new CEO, Lucinda Belliston, developed a buy-back program, where the first-generation models of ALLI's could be returned to the company and replaced with new models of more miniature robots in the home. Everyone took advantage of this opportunity, and few ALLIs that were developed initially remain in existence in Valley Hills. The only ones that are still in operation work mainly at stores as automated tellers or customer service representatives. While these new miniature robots have caused some of the prior conveniences that the ALLIs provided for families to be interrupted, it has also caused a question of the ethical use of technology in homes.

After Lucinda became CEO, a non-profit advocacy group was formed to encourage the use of ProTech technology in the home called HUMAN ALLIES. Their influence has grown as their leader is Caden, a self-proclaimed genius and social media influencer. They often host peaceful protests that draw many teenagers because there will usually be a celebrity to attend. Many of their videos show their protests being at random times and locations to encourage followers to constantly watch their channel. Along with their advocacy for using technology, they also promote the exposure of the Protectors and Caden has even gone to the length to blame the blackouts on them.

Surprisingly, even after Bale's debacle, people in Valley Hills are more open to the theory, as the blackouts have caused significant issues in regard to providing a safe and secure environment. More and more, there have been accidents around the city during the blackouts, with no way of communicating or seeing a resolution outside of using technology. Therefore, any association with the Protectors is now viewed as rebellious to the way of life in Valley Hills, and many of them have had to keep their identities secret.

The city of Valley Hills is preparing for a large celebration hosted by ProTech next week. Belliston stated how it will be the largest celebration in ProTech's history. Plans have been made to host leaders from around the globe to be present for the next revelation from ProTech.

Chapter 11

Breakthrough

The sound of water splashing keeps going through Josh's mind. He can see the splash of water that stopped Noah from attacking his friends and family. He can see the final moments of Noah slip away. He can then hear the splashing of water as his friends were in a line to be baptized. One, after another, being immersed in the water and coming up to loud celebrations and even tears of joy. And yet, he finds himself under the water, swimming for the surface, and yet he gets pulled further and further down, drowning, and gasping for air, time and time again.
"Josh! Wake up!" a voice and shake cause Josh to open his eyes immediately. Josh realizes it is a dream once again, and Terra has his shirt in his hand, shaking him in a whisper. As he comes back to reality, he can hear the others whispering to one another while grasping his mother's cross in his hand.
"Dude, you have got to stop it with the dreaming all the time," Bub says softly in a whisper.
"Wait here a second, I think Yashi is ready to give us the all-clear signal," Terra said.

Then, breaking through the silence, you can hear the whistle similar to the sound of a whippoorwill coming from a set of trees. Josh started to move, and then Bub grabbed his hand and pulled him back down. "Remember we listen for two whistles," Bub said.

The remaining friends pop their heads over the rocks in meerkat fashion to look at the lighthouse entrance, which is just a few feet away. Then, the whistle came again from a set of trees across the path by the road.

"Thank goodness that is done!" Bub said with relief. "I always get a little nervous and gassy at this part. But luckily, I have mastered SBD gas."

"SBD gas?" Terra asked.

"Silent but deadly," Bub replied. "Oh see, there you go." And then, all of a sudden, a smell broke the area that reminded everyone of garbage and rotten eggs.

"Did something die inside of you?" Josh jokingly asked.

"What? I can't help it!" Bub innocently replied with a smirk on his face.

"I could smell you all the way over there!" Yashi says as he emerges from the trees.

"Ok guys, come on, let's get inside," Josh says as they all enter the lighthouse.

Things are different, and the need for secrecy is a way of life for the Protectors. Yet, there are parts that have become normal and provide a sense of security. As the group enters the lighthouse, it is just before the daily devotion is to begin that is led by Thomas. He is starting a study in a new book of the Bible today that he believes the Lord has led him to specifically.

Everyone now calls the Protectors' headquarters, the Den, as there is even a painting of a lion's head on the wall as you enter. The room has both a military headquarters' feel as there are meetings held by the leadership, which now includes Josh's dad, Cal, to discuss security measures for the group. There are also parts of it that feel like a science lab. Different people try to invent new technologies that can help provide security to the Protectors, especially while they are out in Valley Hills.

Josh and the others are even trying to learn how to invent different technologies. Bub has the hardest time with his inventions, mainly because they involve food. He tried to create a cookie that could knock out anyone that smelled it when they opened just the box. Unfortunately, he didn't wear a mask the first time he baked them and passed out from the smell. His latest trial is chewing gum that operates as a listening device that can be placed anywhere, but he still has not mastered it.

The friends talk a lot with Ezzie, a former developer at ProTech, that joined the Protectors after the incident with Bale became public. Ezzie has a great way of encouraging them to try new things. Still, they can also tell that he has a strong knowledge of the Way of the Protectors by how he consistently refers to the Bible. Often times during the church gathering, he and his wife, Desirae, lead the group in a couple of songs about Jesus. Josh always notices the joy on Ezzie and Desirae's faces as they sing, and it inspires him to think about his recent decision to place his faith in Jesus.

As Josh and the others enter the Den, there is always a sense of feeling like this is their true home as they are surrounded by family and friends.

Many of the Protectors still live in Valley Hills and work in different jobs to care for their families. Still, they secretly retreat to the Den at least once a week for their gathering and to celebrate any new members of the Way. Often, music can be heard playing throughout the Den as Ezzie and Desirae prepare to lead the singing time.

The moments of nostalgia and remembrance are suddenly interrupted by what seems to be an argument in what Josh and the friends call the "war room." Josh and the others can discern Cal's voice speaking loudly and can even hear the phrase in a muddled tone, "He is my son and just a boy." Then he hears Aunt Abby speak up in a gentle but firm manner, "Yes, we know that, but he is the key to our survival as Protectors." All the friends look at each other and realize that they are talking about Josh..

Suddenly, the door whips open, and Cal begins to storm out and immediately stops as he notices Josh and his friends standing there. "Well, hey guys! I didn't know you were here," Cal said as he tried to change his tone immediately and to not show his frustration.

"Hey, Dad," Josh said as the group stood there in silence.

Bub immediately tried to change the subject and break the awkward silence that has swept across the Den, "Hey, have ya'll seen Barry's latest video? It's called 'Jumping into Fountains!'"

Bub goes over to a computer and goes to his brother's social media channel, "Adventures with Barry." Since the exposure of Bale, Barry's videos have become viral and have swept across Valley Hills for their humor. Now in the majority of his videos, he is taking online dares from the audience, which includes him being physically hurt in different ways. While Barry sees the dares as being a way to show his toughness, many people laugh at all the different ways that he will hurt himself, and he is oblivious to the way in which people view his popularity.

As the friends are watching the episode, Thomas emerges to the center of the room and says, "It is time to gather friends." Everyone puts away their devices and begins to find their copy of the Bible. Josh usually sits between his father and aunt. Josh can sense the frustration that exists between them. Yet, for a brief moment, the struggles seem to go away as the entire gathering begins to sing as Ezzie leads. Josh can look around the room and see how everyone has their eyes closed, especially his friends, as they are all fully engaged in worship at this moment. It really is something that adds again to the feeling of the Den being his home.

After singing a few songs, Thomas stands up at the front and begins his teaching:

"Today, we are beginning a new series in one of my favorite books in the Bible, Joshua!

Joshua was a man like many of us in this room in that he had more things happening on the inside than on the outside. He wondered what the future would be like. He even had doubts and fears. Think about today; what are the things that you are the most fearful of? What are the things that you doubt? Then ask the question, why? Why do I have doubts? Why do I worry? Once again, Joshua had doubts and fears. You may say, how do I know that Joshua had doubts and fears. Listen to what God said to Joshua when he called him to lead the people. *Be strong and courageous. Do not be afraid; do not be discouraged, for the Lord your*

God will be with you wherever you go. God spoke exactly to who Joshua was on the inside that no one else could see to help him to lead others. He spoke to his doubts and his fears. And the way in which God would carry him through was with His presence. His promise to always be there with Him. Then we go to Jesus' words in Matthew 28, *I am with you, even unto the end of the world.* How does Jesus go with us today, just as God went with Josh? Through the Holy Spirit. Because Jesus is alive today, when we place our faith in Him, we receive the gift of eternal life and the presence of God with us forever in the Holy Spirit! And since God is with us, we can be strong and courageous. We do not need to fear. We do not need to worry. And we simply need to trust in Him! Let's pray."

As Thomas began to pray, Josh could hear his father sniffling. He looked up and could see a tear running down the side of his face. He could look around and see people nodding their heads in agreement with what was being said in the prayer. Yet, he realized that moment the power of the words that were being shared. They spoke to everyone. Yet for Josh, it reminded him of the message regarding his mother and Bale. It reminded him of his friendship with Noah. It reminded him of their hand signal to one another as they would say, "two of everything." It also reminded him that his life was totally different.

At the end of the time, Ezzie stood up and said, "Hey everyone, I am beginning to teach anyone that wants to learn how to sing. You do not have to have any previous singing experience; I really want people that have to help those that have a desire." He began to pass around little flyers that had the dates and times on them when he was going to begin to meet. When Ezzie reached Josh, he made it a point to stop and say, "I really think this would be good for you to try; I can see something inside of you." Josh reluctantly took the flyer and smiled at Ezzie and said, "Thank you."

Chapter 12

System Preferences

Returning to school had mixed emotions for Josh and the others. First, Noah was not there to drop him off anymore. Rather, Josh was dropped off by his father. Often, he was late and rushing to get to his first period. Times were also hard for the friends as more people knew who they were from the events surrounding Bale on that night. The friends had gained some popularity; yet, Tad and his friends, often reminded them that unless he helped them, they would not be alive today. Tad still would play pranks on Josh in front of his friends just to keep up his image to others. It had drawn the attention of Ellie Grace as she and Tad were spending time together outside of school. Furthermore, things were difficult for the friends because they had to keep their identities as being a part of the Protectors a secret. There was once a student version of the group Human Allies that was started in school as a club. In order to promote the club throughout school, students wore shirts with the word 'Protectors' on the front with a big red 'X' across it. When Josh and the others were asked to get a shirt, they came up with excuses to not get one, even to the place where Bub pretend9ed he was sick while being asked to buy one. Many students did not realize what was happening behind the scenes and even made comments similar to what was being said on social media about the Protectors.

The bell rang to begin class. Josh, Yashi, Terra, and Bub were all in the same first period class together with Mr. Rodriguez for English. He always had some saying that was supposed to have been from a famous person in history as a way to start the day.

"Good morning class," Mr. Rodriguez stated to no reply. "Oh, it must have been a long weekend. Not even you, Sir Bub, have a story to share with the class today?"

Bub hated when Mr. Rodriguez called him that. "Okay then," he continued, "well today's quote comes from the famous author Robert Louis Stephenson, 'Sooner or later, we all sit down to a banquet of consequences.' For a moment it seemed as if Mr. Rodriguez was focused on Josh as he said the quote. It was almost as if he knew something was going on in Josh's life that no one was to know.

When it came time to participate in group work, Josh and the friends started to always talk about things happening with the Protectors.

"Guys, I am so close to a breakthrough on my gum invention that also acts as a listening device," Bub said with enthusiasm.

"Oh really," Josh replied with sarcasm.

"I am planning to call it SLUG," as he spread out his hands in front of his face looking to the distance.

"SLUG? Yuck! Who would want to buy gum that is called slugs?" Terra chimed. "You might as well call it Worm Gum. That sounds horrible."

"Why SLUG?" Yashi asked.

"Secret Listening Under Gum," Bub replied with confidence. "Trust me, it will be a hit."

"Yeah right!" Josh replied. All of a sudden, there was a knock at the door and Mrs. Donna, the school secretary that was from Tennessee, walked in and whispered to Mr. Rodriguez and motioned back to the door.

Mrs. Donna then stated in her southern voice, "Now honey, you just come on in here and Mr. Rodriguez will get you a desk for this period." Suddenly, a girl walked in that caught all the guys attention, especially Josh.

Yashi even let out under his breath, "Woah momma!"

"Students," Mr. Rodriguez announced. "If I can have your attention. We have a new student joining us today. Her name is Brittany and she just moved here."

Brittany was noticeably embarrassed by the attention.

Mr. Rodriguez continued, "Brittany, we are in groups of four working on our group work. Does anyone only have three in their group?"

Ellie Grace raised her hand and said, "We only have three! Mr. Rodriguez."

"Great!" Mr. Rodriguez replied, "you can sit next to Ellie Grace and she can help to get you caught up."

As she sat down the low rumble of talking among the students returned while everyone's focus was on Brittany.

"Boys, you can pick up your tongues and put them back in your mouth," Terra said to bring all the guys back to reality.

"Sorry Terra," Bub replied. "I just have never seen someone as beautiful as her before. I think we were meant to be together. It was like one of those moments in a movie that everything slows down and then there she is."

As Terra rolled her eyes, Bub looked up to heaven and motioned with his mouth, "Thank you Lord!"

"Josh…Josh! It's your turn to answer the question on the homework," Yashi said.

Josh was noticeably looking in Brittany's direction and thinking about her, but didn't want to say anything out loud.

"Oh, sorry guys, I was just thinking," Josh hurriedly replied. "What question are we on?"

"Number Two?" Terra said. "But I think you are on the question of the two girls."

"The question of the two girls?" Josh replied in confusion as he grabbed his paper and began to look around it for what Terra was referencing.

"Yeah, the question of which girl are you going to love, Ellie Grace or Brittany?" Terra said sarcastically.

"Whatever!" Josh shrugged off what Terra implied when suddenly he was saved by the bell ringing to end the period.

As students began to rush off, Mr. Rodriguez shouted out, "Don't forget we are out of school for next week's ProTech celebration. Also, Mr. Josh Nunley, I need to see you."

"This can't be good," Josh said under his breath to his friends. "I'll catch up with you all later."

As the class was dismissing, it ended up being that Brittany and Josh were standing at the front alone.

"Ms. Brittany, I hope that you had a good first period with us," Mr. Rodriguez said. "Please let me or Mrs. Donna know of anything we can do to help you here."

"Oh, thank you!" Brittany replied. As she turned around she bumped into Josh standing there and dropped some of her books she had in her hands. Josh reached down to immediately help pick them up. He noticed that one of the books was by a guy named C.S. Lewis and said, "My friend, Terra really enjoys his books," as he tried to make conversation.

"Wow, really! I don't know many people that like his books. Have you read them much?" Brittany replied.

"Uhm yeah, sure," Josh replied knowing he had not read an entire book in the last year.

"Oh, really which one have you read recently?" Brittany asked.

"Uhm, that new one from last year," Josh said, hoping he could escape the conversation.

"Right, right," Brittany replied. "By the way do you know where locker number 318 is?"

"Yeah, 318 is not far from mine," Josh said.

"Ok well that doesn't tell me where it is?" Brittany replied.

"Oh yeah, that's right. By the vending machine in the red hallway," Josh said.

"Thanks!" By the way, what's your name?" Brittany asked.

"Josh," He replied with almost a crack in his voice.

"See you around!" Brittany said as she walked out of the room.

"Are you finished Mr. Nunley?" Mr. Rodriguez said as he interrupted Josh's focus.

"Yes sir," Josh replied embarrassingly not knowing that Mr. Rodriguez was hearing their conversation.

"Listen, the reason that I wanted to talk with you is that your grades are not looking good for this semester. In fact, if you fail one more test, you will have to do extra work to get caught up or you will have to go to summer school," Mr. Rodriguez dropped a bomb on Josh.

"Are you serious?" Josh replied.

"Yes, totally serious?" Mr. Rodriguez said. "I would like to talk with your dad if that is possible to make sure he is aware of the situation."

Josh knew that talking to his dad would mean less time that he would be able to spend at the Den helping the Protectors. He scrambled over what to reply, "Can I stay after school and do some make up work?" Knowing that his dad would not miss him for a few extra minutes.

"Josh I am sorry but it is beyond that point. I am sending him this note home with you for you to give it to him so that we can set up a time to discuss what's happening with your grades," Mr. Rodriguez said. "Josh I care about your success in academics and I know you are a bright kid; I just can see there are some things that seem to have your attention that seem to be distractions."

"Yes sir," Josh said as he hung his head and started to leave the room.

"By the way," Mr. Rodriguez stopped Josh. "Be careful out there."

Josh was confused by the comment and simply looked at Mr. Rodriguez and said, "Thank you."

As he left, his friends had already gone to their next class. But Josh walked slowly almost in a daze about what Mr. Rodriguez meant by his comment. The questions began to run through Josh's mind. Did he know that they were Protectors? Was he a secret Protector? What was he going to do about his grades? What would his dad do to him? And then Josh began to think, how can I spend more time with Brittany?

As the bell rang to get to the next class, Josh snapped back and realized he was going to be late to his next class. He took off running and came around the corner, when his feet went out from under neath him and in a moment when he felt like he was suspended in the air for an eternity, he fell on his back. Unfortunately, it happened right in front of Tad and his fellow football players, as well as Ellie Grace.

"Wow! Slow down, Usain Bolt!" Tad said loudly and with sarcasm. "Why the rush?"

Through the pain and embarrassment, Josh rolled on his stomach and tried to stand back up again in a hurry and slipped again to fall to his knees and hands.

Tad and his friends began to point their fingers and laugh and say, "Thanks Nunley, I needed a great laugh today."

Ellie Grace broke through Tad and the guys and tried to help Josh stand back up. "Leave him alone." Ellie Grace sternly directed to Tad and the guys. "Sorry they are being mean."

"I got it, I got it!" Josh quietly said as he tried to stand to his feet without Ellie Grace's assistance. As Ellie Grace tried to help him, he looked at her and said sternly, "Ellie Grace, I got it."

Ellie Grace backed up from Josh with a shocked look on her face. She had never heard him talk that way to her before and she was confused as she hurried away with tears on her face. Tad stepped forward to Josh and puffed up his chest and said, "Be careful how you talk to Ellie Grace bro!" He then leaned into Josh's ear and whispered, "You may think she used to be yours, but she is mine now. Got it!"

Josh pulled back and looked at Tad's eyes and said, "Got it!"

As Tad and his friends walked away laughing, a large man came rushing forward suddenly. "Are you okay, son?" he stated in a low bellowing voice.

Josh looked behind him and saw a large man with a concerned look on his face. It was the janitor. "I'm so sorry, I had just mopped this floor and didn't have my sign out yet," he said as he was trying to apologize for his error. "Here let me help you pick up these papers, son."

As they scurried around to pick up papers, Josh looked down and saw the name on the shirt of the janitor, "Tim." As they both stood up, Tim looked at him again and said, "Are you sure you are okay? You don't need to see the school nurse?" For a moment, Josh had a feeling like he was being cared for by Noah. He remembered the times when Noah came along and helped him when he fell off his bike or while playing outside. "Son, are you ok?"

As Josh snapped back to reality and to try to avoid further embarrassment he quickly replied, "I am good. Thanks for your help," as he began to walk away, suddenly the bell rang and he realized he was late to his next class, which meant detention.

Chapter 13

Search Engine

Detention was held in the library each afternoon after school. For Josh, this was a familiar setting as his father was often late in getting him to school. Most of the time it gave Josh a chance to catch up on any homework before going home so he could focus on matters for the Protectors. Today, however, his head was swimming with thoughts of Mr. Rodriguez's statement, Brittany, Ellie Grace, and Tad. The things running through his head became overwhelming so he thought he would try to hide his face and take a nap. Mrs. Donna, the school secretary, supervised detention in the library, which meant for her and she got to spend time on social media on her phone. Since her focus was on her phone, as long as you were quiet, you could do whatever you wanted. You could even walk around the library as long as it looked like you were searching for books.

Josh was just about to lay down his head when a large book suddenly slammed on the table right next to him. It was Sylvester. Sylvester was the poster-boy for school nerds and was known for his ability to offer useless information through what seemed to be a consistent issue with allergies and thick glasses. Josh and Sylvester were in the same science class even though Josh often sat on the other side of the room. Sylvester's ability to share useless information however often got him into trouble for talking in class as he would often correct the teacher and he would be given detention.

"Well, hello Mr. Nunley," Sylvester said through a sniffle, while he pushed his glasses further up his nose. "Fancy to see you here again. Late again I suppose."

"Hey Sylvester," Josh said reluctantly. "I really want to take a nap if that's ok."

"Yes, Josh that is fine. I am going to just sit here and read my book on physics," Sylvester inquired.

"Yes that is fine Sylvester. Just let me sleep," Josh said sluggishly to try and encourage Sylvester to stop talking.

Suddenly, a roaring "Shh," came from Mrs. Donna as she was staring at Josh and Sylvester and finished with pointing her finger at Josh.

Josh look frustrated, realizing that Mrs. Donna apparently thought that Josh was the only one talking.

Without missing a beat Sylvester continued, "By the way Josh, did you know that these blackouts happening all over the city are a strange phenomenon?"

"Really?" Josh said with his face planted into his folded arms on the library table.

"Oh yes!" Sylvester continued. "My dad says that there is no reason that we should have these blackouts. We have a strong power grid! We have the most efficient technology. He says that there is a conspiracy behind these blackouts."

"Really?" Josh replied again from his napping position.

Suddenly, the southern voice of Mrs. Donna, rang out from the front of the library, "Mr. Nunley, honey, you need to be quiet or I will make you stay an extra hour."

Confused again by how Mrs. Donna thought Josh was the sole culprit, he tried to direct Mrs. Donna's attention to Sylvester. Yet her only response was to hold her finger over his lips with a threatening look. Immediately after Mrs. Donna began to look at her phone again. Sylvester continued his monologue about the blackouts. Josh realized that he was not going to get any sleeping done while Sylvester was there, so he thought that the next best tactic was to do homework so that Sylvester would leave him alone. He reached into his bookbag and began to pull out papers, giving occasional head nods and "Oh really" statements to Sylvester, while not paying attention to what he was saying. Realizing that he hadn't organized any of the papers after his fall in the hallway, he thought about looking for Mr. Rodriguez's note again to consider how to talk to his dad about his grades.

As he pulled more papers and books out of his bag, he realized that the note was not there. He began to frantically look around his table and chair in the library, hoping that it had fallen on the ground around him. He began to look through all his books. Nothing. He then began to then take his books and turn them upside down and shake them to try and see if the note was stuck in between some pages. Suddenly, a small bright orange piece of paper fell out of one of the books. He realized that he had not put that paper in his books. When he picked it up, he saw that it said "J. Nunley" on one side and he turned it over to read:

LD331-TOE

"LD331-TOE?" Josh said under his breath. He began to look around to see if anyone was looking for him. Sylvester had already changed his topic of conversation to what he was reading in his physics book. Josh wondered if he may have picked up the wrong science book. So, he looked at Sylvester and interrupted his talk, "Hey Sylvester, was this note yours?"

Sylvester looked at it for a brief moment and said quickly, "Nope! Not mine!" Josh sat back confused again.

"But it looks like you wrote down a book to find," Sylvester replied.

"What?" Josh asked.

"Yeah that is a library call number," Sylvester said.

"What is?" Josh asked again.

"LD331," Sylvester said. "Don't you know the Dewey Decimal System?"

"Uhm..." Josh replied searching for what to ask without sounding too dumb.

"It looks like a number that is referencing a book here in the library. It even has the author's initials, TOE," Sylvester said.

"So, all I have to do is use those numbers and I should find a book?" Josh asked.

"Yes," Sylvester replied with sarcasm. "And people say that I am the dumb one."

Josh began to look around the room and could start to see the letters and numbers at the end of each aisle of books. He saw aisle J, then K. but he couldn't find L. He looked at Sylvester and asked, "Where is section L?"

"Section L is in the back of the library," as Sylvester motioned in a direction. "Not many people go back there however just because the books are not any good there."

Josh got up and grabbed his books and papers, stuffed them in his bag, and began to walk back in the direction that Sylvester motioned. He carried the piece of paper in his hand and suddenly came across section L. It was dusty and even had a different smell from most of the other parts of the library that were filled with computers.

As he began to walk down the aisle looking through the numbers, he finally began to see the letters matching up of L and then D. He began to scroll across the books with his fingers and he saw 328, then 329, then 330, and then, there it was, LD331. The book was different from the others in that it looked older. He looked at the title and it read, "Boats."

"Boats?" Josh whispered to himself again. He stared for a moment at the ground, wondering where the note came from and why this book on boats. He then turned the book over and saw written across the pages, "Protec tRUTH." He was confused about the spelling.

Suddenly, Josh felt a hand on his shoulder. He let out a little yell, "Ahh," that was copied by Sylvester that had followed him. As they both stood there for a moment, gasping for air, Sylvester reached into his pocket and pulled out his asthma inhaler and gave a quick pump of air into his lungs to calm him down.

"What are you doing Sylvester?" Josh asked.

"I wanted to come and help," Sylvester replied as he continued to gasp for air. "What's that?" he asked.

"It's just a book about boats. It looks like an old book," Josh said as he was turning it over.

"Protect Truth, what does that mean?" Sylvester asked as he began to reach for the book.

Josh pulled back the book out of Sylvester's reach and sharply replied, "I'm sure it's nothing."

Confused, Josh and Sylvester returned to their seats. He put the book down on the table and began to wonder why he was given a note that would lead him to find this book.

"Boats are interesting," Josh could see that this was the beginning of another useless information rant by Sylvester. "They are buoyant, which means they push against water, and its determined by its weight and volume."

"Shh, keep it down, Sylvester," Josh whispered, as he noticed Mrs. Donna beginning to look up from her phone.

"Do you know one of the first boats ever in history?" Sylvester asked.

"Noah's ark," Sylvester said. "Could you imagine being able to get two of every animal on that boat?"

While Sylvester was talking, Josh noticed how Sylvester was pulling his fingers across the pages of the books. Josh noticed a dark spot in the middle while the pages were moving. He suddenly stopped Sylvester and grabbed the book from his hands. He realized that there was more to this book that he originally thought.

He looked again at the cover of the book and noticed that the author's name was Noah Arkeson. Then he looked again at the spine and saw the full call number to be LD331, TOE-G6.

"TOE" Two of Everything," Josh said.

"Yes, that's how many animals Noah put on the ark," Sylvester stated.

He flipped it over and opened the book and started to go through the pages, when finally, there was a page he flipped over and there was an empty spot that had been cut out.

Josh turned the next page slowly and there was a section of the book with cut out pages that acted like a secret hiding place and there was a small piece of paper folded.

"Wow," Sylvester said, "I have never seen that before."

Josh motioned to Sylvester to be quiet as they both began to look around to see if anyone else could see their discovery.

"You have to read what it says," Sylvester said softly.

Josh slowly started to unfold the small piece of paper while Sylvester cautiously watched. Josh began to have a rush of questions going through his mind: Why this book? What's this going to say? Is this about my mother? Suddenly, a hand was put on their shoulders that surprised them. Josh, Sylvester, and Mrs. Donna all let out a yell in surprise. Sylvester was so shocked that he passed out immediately and fell forward on the table and lied there limp.

"Go and get cold, wet paper towels," Mrs. Donna barked at Josh. Josh ran to the bathroom and wet some paper towels and brought them back to see Sylvester slowly moaning and regaining consciousness. Mrs. Donna was holding a piece of paper in her hand like a fan trying to revive Sylvester. She kept repeating with her southern accent, "Sylvester, honey, are you ok?" She grabbed the paper towels from Josh's hand and began to announce to all the students, "Ok everyone, due to circumstances, detention is over. You can all go home." She looked at Josh and said, "Mr. Nunley, I need to call his parents and let him know what happened. Please wait here while I go call them."

While Mrs. Donna stepped away, Josh stood there, not really knowing what to do, except to try and get Sylvester's attention. "Hey man. You, ok?" Sylvester continued to groan and Josh could see a big bump coming up on Sylvester's forehead from where he must have hit his head. His glasses even looked broken in the middle. Josh looked down and whispered to Sylvester, "I'm sorry man for this. I'll let you know what the message says."
Mrs. Donna returned to Sylvester and Josh and said, "His parents are on the way. By the way, what were you all looking at?"

Josh thought he needed to not say anything about the paper and said, "We were reading about boats."

Mrs. Donna reached down to pick up the book and started to run her fingers through the book as she said, "It must have been a good book to have both of your attention like that."

Josh realized what she could find, so he immediately grabbed the book from Mrs. Donna and said, "Well it's important homework. Thanks for asking," as he grabbed his bag and quickly left the library.

Chapter 14

The Code

Cal decided that after the events with Noah and with the memory of Deborah, Josh's mother, being so heavy in their previous home that it was best for them to live with Aunt Abby, Uncle Ty, and their new baby Bradley temporarily. Aunt Abby and Ty's recognized that life for Josh was difficult with Cal's attention now being on helping the Protectors. They often acted like parents for Josh as they were present in his life, while they also tried to let Cal be the voice of authority in his life as his father.

Previously, Josh's life was furnished with every technology available to provide an ease of life while Cal worked at ProTech, however, in their new current living arrangements, life looked much different. For Abby and Ty, technology was used but only if it was not connected to a network. They rarely went to a store or spent money using cards as Aunt Abby and Ty focused on producing their own food with a garden and small farm animals running around the yard. They would sell a lot of their vegetables and food to other Protectors (they often gave extra vegetables and fruit to older Protectors), and then outside of Valley Hills at local farmer markets to earn money. Their lives were simplistic and they loved it. Their form of entertainment involved Aunt Abby dancing and holding Bradley while Ty played the ukulele. Josh fortunately was able to have his own room as this was originally planned to be the baby room for Bradley.

After the events in the library, Josh rushed into the house and ran upstairs to his room and closed the door. He bypassed Aunt Abby and Uncle Ty, sitting in the den playing with Bradley with a quick "Hey I have a lot of homework." As he sat there confused and working through many questions in his mind, he heard a slight knock on the door followed by it slowly being opened. It was Uncle Ty as he said softly, "Josh? Josh?"

"Hey Uncle Ty," Josh replied. "Sorry that I rushed by."

"No worries," Ty said in a cool softened voice. "I do need your help with some chores when you get done with your homework. We have a big crop that we need to take to the next city for this weekend and I need your help."

"Yes sir," Josh replied. "By the way, have you heard from my dad?"

Ty looked down, "No sorry Josh, I have not. But I will keep trying. Finish up that homework quickly though."

"Yes sir," Josh replied.

Josh waited for Ty to close the door when he rushed over to his bag and pulled out the book on boats. He slowly began to turn its pages to where he reached the small piece of paper again. He pulled it out and began to slowly open it. On the paper he found written:

"40 days are over. 40 nights are not. The Rose has bloomed, remember where one was not, one is now. Two know where one is but not one."

He sat there perplexed by what he just read and the questions began again: What did it mean? Was this really meant for him?

He thought that the best thing he could do was to show it to the other friends and see what they thought. The group began to use a series of radios that could not be picked up by anyone else. Often, Josh would send a message to the group via social media with the statement, CB-19, which was code for them to get on the radio. After sending out the message, he began to talk on his radio and say a code for the group, "Noah coming in, Anyone out there? Over." He said it again to see if there was any response.

Suddenly, a noise started to break through the silence, "This is Twinkie, Noah. Over." Twinkie was Bub's name on the radio. Then another sound came through, "This is Soul Man. Over," as Yashi joined the discussion. Finally, the voice they all anticipated came through, "Terra is here. Over." Josh realized that Terra hated the nicknames so he replied back sarcastically, "I'm sorry, you were breaking up, I didn't get that official name."

"Do I have to say it?" Terra replied in frustration.

"We can only talk on here with code names," Yashi replied. "It protects our identity."

"Fine," Terra said followed by a moment of silence. Then in a whispered voice she replied, "This is Earth Girl. Over."

"I'm sorry, I didn't get that" Bub replied sarcastically.

"Don't push it. What's up Noah?" Terra asked.

"Can you all meet at the spot? I have big news. The biggest news of all," Josh said with full excitement.

"Yeah, I can be there at 7 tonight." Yashi replied.

"Sounds good to me!" Josh said. "How about Twinkie and Earth Girl? Over."

"Twinkie will be there; do I need to bring snacks?" Bub asked.

"No, just be there," Josh replied. "What about you Earth Girl? Over." As the group waited again after a moment of silence, Terra's voice came through, "I'll be there."

Yashi quickly asked, "Who is this again? Over."

"Don't push it. I'll be there. Over," Terra replied with frustration in her voice.

At dinner, Aunt Abby looked at Josh and said, "So I noticed you were late getting home today from school. Did you have detention again?"

Josh hung his head and replied, "Yes, but it wasn't my fault. You see, I fell in the hallway and dropped all my papers and when I..." Josh paused for a second as he realized that the paper could have only gotten there from the janitor.

"You what?" Ty asked. "They gave you a detention for falling. I have heard school is tough, but I didn't know that you couldn't fall. I mean I guess you could fail but not fall." Ty began to chuckle as his own joke. Abby rolled her eyes and smirked but then came back to Josh, "What do you mean you fell?"

Josh, realizing that he had been asked a question, returned to the conversation, "Uhm yeah, I mean, I slipped in the hallway and was late to my class and the teacher didn't like that so he gave me a detention. I'm sorry."

"Isn't that like your fifth or sixth detention this year?" Aunt Abby asked. "That does not sound good. Are you ok?"

"Yeah, I'm fine. By the way, what time is it?" Josh asked.

"6:45," Ty said.

"6:45? I'll be late," Josh stood up and ran upstairs to get the book.

When he came downstairs, he was met by Aunt Abby holding Bradley. "Josh, where are you running off to? Ty had some chores for you to help him with."

"I'm sorry, Aunt Abby, this is extremely important. I have to go," Josh replied as he tried to move past her.

"Where are you going young man? "Abby replied in a sterner tone.

Josh looked down and saw the book in his hand and quicky said, "I have to work on a book report. It's a report on boats."

"A book report on boats?" Abby said. "What book is it?" As she leaned forward to see the book in his hand.

Josh quickly pulled back and ran out the door and grabbed his bicycle to head to the spot.

He rushed by Ty that said, "Josh, what about these chores?"

Josh sped away knowing that Abby and Ty were upset with what he just did. He was upset with himself as well that he felt that he had to lie to them to get out of the conversation.

When Josh arrived at the spot, Terra and Bub were already there. Terra's arms were folded as Josh could tell that she was upset from the earlier conversation on the radio as well as Bub's rambling. Bub was trying to get her to tell him ways that he could see if Brittany liked him.

"Where's Yashi?" Josh asked. "I really need his help."

Suddenly, breaking through the trees, Yashi, came riding up, almost out of breath.

"I really hate the Turner's dogs," Yashi said through his gasps for breath.

"So, what's so important? What is this big news?" Terra asked.

"This?" Josh said confidently as he held up his hand with the piece of paper.

"What is that?" Bub asked. "A love note from Ellie Grace?"

The others all let out a crescendo of "Woo" followed by kissing sounds.

"No guys! This is the key to finding my mother," Josh replied.

"What do you mean?" Yashi asked.

"So, when I was at detention, I began looking for a note for my dad and couldn't find it. Then this paper fell out of one of my books," Josh began to pass around the orange piece of paper for them all to see. "Then I realized that it was a number for one of the books in the library."

"You realized this on your own?" Yashi asked sarcastically.

"Ok, ok, so I had some help from Sylvester," Josh said. "But I went and found this book. Then when I opened it up, I found that it had a secret compartment in the pages and there was this note."

Josh then held up the note again and slowly unfolded it and they all began to read it out loud:

"40 days are over. 40 nights are not. The Rose has bloomed, remember where one was not, one is now. Two know where one is but not one."

"What does it mean?" Bub asked.

"I don't know," Josh replied. "But I think it is a clue."

"A clue about what?" Terra asked.

"A clue about my mom?" Josh replied.

Josh noticed the silence in the group and looked around and could see the friends looking at each other suspiciously.

"What's wrong?" Josh asked.

"Josh," Terra began to speak softly. "We want you to be careful."

"What do you mean? Careful about what?" Josh sharply replied.

"Josh, we just don't want you to get hurt," Yashi said.

"Why would I get hurt?" Josh asked.

"We just know that you have been down this road before of searching for your mother and it has ended in dead ends and you get hurt," Yashi said.

"You are my friends," Josh replied with tears. "If there is anyone that should be able to help me, it should be you. If there is anyone that should believe me, it should be you."

The group sat silent for a moment as Josh began to cry.

"I'm with you!" Bub said as he moved towards Josh and turned towards Yashi and Terra.

"Oh, you don't have to..." Josh said.

"No! You are my friend! We have been through things and if this means that we need to be here again for one another. We will do it! I will do it! We are Protectors remember. And that means we protect each other!" Bub said with an inspiring confidence.

"Thanks man!" Josh said.

"You are right!" Yashi chimed in. "Josh I will be here for you as well." As he moved over to stand with Bub and Josh and they looked back at Terra.

"You know this is crazy!" Terra said.

They all looked at each other and in unison began to nod their heads.

"But I guess we will be crazy together!" She said as a smile came across her face. The group moved forward and had a moment of an embrace.

"You know who needs to see this?" Josh asked.

"Who?" they responded in unison.

"Ezzie," Josh replied.

"I don't know if I want to get the Protectors involved in this," Terra replied.

"If you don't get them involved, how can they help? This message may affect them just as much as it affects me," Josh replied.

"Yeah, but you know they do not want us to get involved," Terra said. "For all we know, this is just someone playing a joke on you. It could be Tad."

"No, it's too elaborate for Tad and his goons." Yashi said.

"Let's make a deal. We will talk with Ezzie alone and not tell anyone else about it," Josh said.

"Fine but be careful," Terra replied.

"Great, let's meet there tomorrow after school," Josh said.

"You really believe she's really out there," Terra looked at Josh and asked.

"Yeah, I really believe that she is," Josh replied. "I don't know where, but I feel that she is reaching out to me. I just wish she would just pop out and say here I am."

"Ok then, let's find you mother," Terra said.

Josh returned home and thought that everyone had forgotten about what happened earlier and thought he could just rush up to his room. As he entered the front door, he was met by Ty standing at the door. He had never seen this type of look on Ty's face and it was not good. He looked at Josh and said, "Josh, let's sit down and have a talk." Josh's stomach sank as he realized that he had been caught in his lie.

"Josh, I know that you lied to us," Ty said. "My biggest question is why?"

"I'm sorry about lying about going to study," Josh said, "I really am sorry, I went to go and see my friends."

"I'm not talking about that. I am talking about the problems you are having in English class with Mr. Rodriguez. He called your dad tonight about your recent grades and a note to meet but you didn't show it to anyone," Ty said.

Josh realized in that moment that he had totally forgotten about the note in the midst of everything that had happened. He tried to offer an excuse. "Yes, I am sorry I forgot about that note. I…"

Ty cut him off, "Son, you didn't just forget about it, I feel like the way that you have been acting, that you intentionally chose to not tell us. We have to have trust among us. We want to trust you and help you, but things like this hurt that trust between us. Then, when you don't do your chores and help in the family, it hurts us all. Now, to know that you lied to us when you left tonight, hurts things again."

Josh realized that the battle was not worth it. "Yes I am sorry."

Ty said, "You have to remember that with our choices there are consequences. While I am not your father, you are living in our house with our rules. So, your father and us agreed that you are to be grounded for two weeks or until you can show your improvement on your English tests. The only place that you will be able to go to is the Den."

"But I need to be able to see my friends, we have something important that we are working on," Josh replied.

"What's so important that you have to argue about consequences of lying?" Ty asked.

Josh remembered the pact that the group made to keep things silent and simply replied, "You wouldn't understand."

Ty suspiciously looked at Josh and asked, "Are you sure there isn't something else that you need to tell us?"

Josh hung his head and said, "Yes sir."

Ty then said, "Ok, off to bed. It's straight to and from school for the next two weeks and no detention or things will get extended. Do you understand?"

Josh said, "Yes sir."

Chapter 15

Decoding

The next morning, Josh awoke to the smell of his favorite breakfast food, pancakes. His excitement soon was overshadowed by the realization that this was the beginning of a long time of being grounded. He knew that he had to get to the Den to talk to Ezzie to continue moving forward in his investigation. As he sat there at the breakfast table eating his pancakes, Ty came in the kitchen, "Good morning to my favorite garden worker!" Josh knew that this meant that Ty and Abby had a list of chores a mile long to get through on that day. Josh moaned under his breath at the thought of working outside all day.

He crashed his head down on the table as he took his last bite, realizing that the work was about to begin. He then slowly began to open his eyes and could see under some papers the flyer that Ezzie gave him about learning how to sing. He popped his head up and asked Ty, "What day is it?"

"It's Saturday," Ty replied in confusion.

"No, I mean what is the date?" Josh asked hurriedly.

"It's March 25th," Ty replied.

"Josh reached over and grabbed the paper and exclaimed to Ty, "I have singing practice with Ezzie today."

"Singing practice?" Ty asked. "What do you mean, singing practice?"

"You said that the only place I could go to was the Den. And this is at the Den and it seems like Ezzie needs my help. He did stop and say that this would be good for me to attend," Josh replied.

Abby came into the room to fill up her coffee cup, when Ty asked, "Did you know that Josh has singing practice today?"

"Singing practice?" Abby asked in the same tone of confusion. "I know that Ezzie needs some help and we did say that Josh could go to the Den."

Ty looked at Josh and could see the excitement on his face. "Ok, you can go, but you come straight home after singing practice."

Josh ran upstairs to change, "Thank you, thank you!" he exclaimed.

Ty and Abby were both stunned and Abby said, "I have never seen that boy more excited to sing!"

Josh ran into his room and got on the radio, "Twinkie, Soul Man, and Earth Girl, this is Noah. Can you hear me? Over."

"This is Twinkie, over," Bub said with what sounded like a full mouth of food.

"Soul Man here, over," Yashi replied.

"Earth Girl here, over," Terra said in a slow sarcastic tone.

Josh said, "Meet me at the Den. Over. Oh, and by the way, be ready to sing."

Almost immediately all responded in unison, "Sing?"

Ezzie was excited to see how Josh and his friends were the ones that showed up to his singing practice time. He began, "How many of you enjoy singing?"

At first there was silence, then Yashi slowly raised his hand. Ezzie excitedly asked, "Mr. Yashi, you enjoy singing?"

Yashi replied, "Well not really, I enjoy hearing other people sing like Bub." Bub realized that Yashi was playing a joke on him.

"Oh, Mr. Bub, I didn't know you were such a singer. Usually when you are here in service, I do not hear you singing," Ezzie asked.

Bub slowly replied, "Well, I do enjoy singing in the shower and my mom has to ask me to stop all the time, so I guess I can sing really loud."

Ezzie dropped his head, "So, none of you can sing?"

The friends turned towards each other and slowly began to shake their heads.

"So, what gives guys? Why did you come here today?" Ezzie replied.

Josh spoke up, "Ezzie, it's my fault. I am sorry that we came here to meet you like this. The reality is that we can't sing. But we need your help. I think that there is someone trying to tell me something about my mother. And this was the only way that I thought we could talk with you alone."

Ezzie looked at Josh and his friends and could see their anticipation of what he would say next. "So, you lied to your family to come here and talk to me. I do not know if I want to be a part of this."

Josh replied, "Ezzie, I promise that we will all go tell our family when we are finished here today. This was so important and I really need your help."

"Guys, I can't be a part of this. Please go home and tell your family now." Ezzie said.

Saddened by his response, the group began to walk up the stairs. "Come on guys, we will get someone else to help with the code," Josh said to all the friends.

As they were walking out of the Den, Terra looked at Josh and asked, "So who is going to help us with understanding the code?"

"I don't know. I guess it's back to being grounded," Josh sadly said. As the friends came out of the lighthouse and began to ride off on their bikes, suddenly they could hear a voice behind them yelling, "Did you say a code?" It was Ezzie! He began to conspicuously look around and said, "Hurry everyone, come back inside immediately, we have to talk."

After Josh explained the series of events over the past few days, immediately Ezzie raised his hand as if to silence Josh.

"What does it mean Ezzie?" Josh broke through the silence. Ezzie raised his hand again as he leaned back in his chair with a grin on his face.

"There is someone special from the past that is trying to get in contact with you Josh," Ezzie said. "But before I tell you who it is, I need to talk with your dad and some of the others."

"Why do you have to talk to them?" Josh asked, "It's my message, shouldn't I be able to know who it is from?"

"It's not that simple, Josh," Ezzie said. "You see, before you knew about this place, we had to communicate through different ways in order to not be found out. When Bale realized we were doing this, he tried to put a stop to it. But we kept finding ways to communicate messages often in code. Since Bale knows about how we do messages, my fear is that he could be using this as a way to get to you."

"But there is still the possibility that it could be a message about or even from my mother, right?" Josh asked. "She knows how you all communicated as well and she could be trying to reach me."

"I don't know Josh," Ezzie said with hesitancy. "The question for us is why now and why you? I need to talk with Thomas, Cal, and Abby. The key between now and then is to make sure that you do not tell anyone else about this book or message. Is there anyone else that knows about it?

"Well, the only other person that saw me with the book and message is Sylvester," Josh said.

"Sylvester?" Bub asked, "Like annoying Sylvester from school?"

"He was in detention with me and helped me find the book," Josh said.

"Did he see the message?" Ezzie asked.

"No, I found it later," Josh said. "In fact, he passed out."

"So, there was no one else watching you?" Ezzie asked.

"No, I am sure of it," Josh said.

The next day was Sunday and Josh went to the Den with his family for their gathering. As normal, Ezzie and Desirae led in singing and Thomas delivered the message for the day. The message that day happened to be on Daniel in the lion's den, one of Yashi's favorite. He loved the part when the lions were silent while Daniel was in the den being brave.

After the service, Ezzie came to Cal, Abby, and Josh and asked if he could talk to them privately. When they walked in the room, Thomas was there as well waiting. Cal asked, "Are we having a meeting? If so, Josh doesn't need to be in here!"

"Yes he is to be in here!" Ezzie said. "It involves him specifically as he has something that he needs to share with everyone. Go ahead Josh."

Josh then told the story again about the book and read to them the clue that he found inside.

"40 days are over. 40 nights are not. The Rose has bloomed, remember where one was not, one is now. Two know where one is but not one."

"Son, why didn't you share this with us?" Cal asked in frustration.

"I wanted to, but I also got in trouble over my grades and being in detention. So, I didn't have a chance to share what happened. Aunt Abby and Uncle Ty, I also lied to you. The only reason that I came to singing practice was to ask Ezzie about the code. I am sorry," Josh said as he hung his head.

Thomas spoke up, "Josh, The Lord has a way of taking our messes and using them for His purpose. I remember a lady in Scripture that was a mess and yet God used her to save the children of Israel. Her name was Rahab and if you look in the Bible today, you will see that she is a part of Jesus' lineage. It doesn't mean that we try to make more messes, but He shows us how His way is always better than our way."

"Dad, I am sorry as well," Josh said to his dad. "I realize that you are under a lot of pressure and I want to help and not be a problem."

"Son, you are never a problem!" Cal said as he embraced Josh.

"Seems that the Lord is already using this for His glory," Thomas said. "So, what now?"

"I think we need to forget about this." Cal said. "I think this is an old message that was found in a book the Protectors used that Josh stumbled across."

"My fear is that this is Bale," Abby spoke up. "I think he could be using the system to isolate Josh in some way and to come after all of us."

"What do you think?" Thomas said to Ezzie.

"I am not sure," Ezzie said in confusion. "I feel that there are more questions than answers right now and that bothers me. The answer is in the code, but I don't know how yet." He got up and began to read over the message again and he would close his eyes as if he was thinking more and more.

Josh spoke up, "I really believe that the message is from mom."

Cal began to comfort Josh, "Son we just don't know that and we have said before that everything points to her not being alive more than he being here still."

"I know Dad, but Thomas always says that faith is believing in those things we can't see. While I can't see Mom, I believe she is out there. I have faith that she is. I have faith that she is trying to talk to me now," Josh said.

Suddenly Ezzie asked, "Josh, do you happen to have the book with you?"

"The book?" Cal asked, "What does that have to do with the message?"

"It may be a help to us," Ezzie explained.

"No, I left it in my room at home," Josh said, "Why?"

"Josh, is there anything else that you remember about the book?" Ezzie asked.

"Not really, it was a book about boats with the middle cut out," Josh replied.

"Was there anything written around it?" Ezzie asked.

"All I remember written across the pages was the words, 'Protect truth,'" Josh said.

"Was 'truth' written in all capitals?" Ezzie asked.

"How did you know?" Josh said in amazement.

Ezzie shouted, "That's it!"

"What's it?" Abby asked.

Ezzie walked over to an old chalkboard in the room and wrote down the words as they were on the pages, "Protec tRUTH."

"No, no, no," Cal said. "Someone is playing with our minds."

"What does it mean?" Josh asked as he was confused.

"It has to be her," Thomas said, "Who else could it be?"

"But that's impossible. She is dead. She died in the accident," Cal said.

"You remember how we always questioned the reports," Thomas said. "This may be her way of saying that she is alive and that the only person that would believe her is Josh."

"I knew this message is from mom," Josh said.

"No Josh, it's not from your mom," Ezzie said. "It's about your grandmother, Ruth."

Chapter 16

Following

The next day at school as Josh was leaving his last class with Bub, Yashi, and Terra, he came out of the doors and bumped immediately into Brittany causing her to drop some of her books.
"Oh, I'm sorry," Josh said as reached down to help her pick up the books. "I guess we need to stop bumping into each other like this." As soon as the words left his mouth, he realized how cheesy it sounded.
"I don't mind," Brittany said. "If you can just wear a bell around that way I know where you are and to get out of the way."
"Yeah will do," Josh said as Brittany slowly walked away.
"Back to earth Mr. Nunley," Bub began to say in a robot voice.
"Leave me alone guys," Josh said in embarrassment.
"I heard that she only likes smart guys," Yashi said with a smirk of confidence.
"Hey the girl has to eat!" Bub said as he and Yashi walked out of the doors.
"Ok, please stop, before I vomit," Terra exclaimed.
"I need to grab something out of my locker," Josh said.
"I'll wait for you," Terra said.

As Josh walked to his locker, he noticed how Ellie Grace was at her locker as well. She gave him a wave and said, "Hey Josh, I hope you are doing good."

He stopped and began to talk to her, "Hey Ellie Grace, where's Tad?"

"Tad and I stopped talking to one another. I realized how much I need good friends more than a boyfriend in my life," Ellie Grace said.

"That's good that you need friends," Josh replied as he continued to think of things to say.

"By the way, have you seen the new movie about the aliens that is coming out?" Ellie Grace said.

"No, I am sorry, I haven't, I have been pretty busy and grounded," Josh said.

"Oh man, I am sorry about that. I hope it's not too much longer," Ellie Grace said. "Maybe we can all hang out as friends soon."

Josh's attention suddenly was interrupted as Terra leaned over and said, "Josh, isn't that the janitor from the other day, Tim? I wonder if he knows about the message."

Josh looked up and could see Tim mopping the floor.

Josh said to Ellie Grace, "I am sorry I have to go. I'll talk to you soon about aliens."

Ellie Grace stood there shocked at the immediate ending of the conversation.

Josh and Terra began to follow Tim, trying to not be seen. After he put up his mop, he came out of the closet and looked both ways trying to see if anyone was watching him. Josh and Terra slid back behind some lockers to not be seen. They noticed that he bypassed the parking lot and began to walk down the street, stopping every now and then to see if anyone was watching him.

Josh and Terra followed far behind him where they couldn't be seen. Suddenly they noticed that he crossed the street and entered a house that was a part of some of the first homes in Valley Hills. Often these homes had some of the older people in Valley Hills that were a part of the first workers for ProTech. The house that he went into stood out different from the other homes in that it looked like an older home similar to those found on a farm. Josh and Terra slipped behind the bushes across the street.

"Why did he go into that house? Who is he?" Terra asked.

"I don't know but I have to find out," Josh said. "I am going to go over there and just see if anything stands out and then I will come back. Wait here and if I am not back in 15 minutes, call my dad."

"Ok, be careful," Terra said.

Josh began to sneak across the street, trying to hide his head down as he had seen on videos beforehand. He noticed immediately that the house was not like others in that there were not perimeter cameras or drones flying around. He slipped to the side of the house and tried to look into the window, but couldn't see anything as there were blinds over the windows.

He suddenly heard a man's voice began to say, "Well the boy was good today." Josh noticed that the voice seemed to move towards the next room of the house that was further back in the house.

Josh looked over at Terra as she was hiding and motioned for her to wait as if to say that he was going to keep watching.

Josh moved towards the next set of windows and as he began to slip his head up to catch a view. Suddenly the man was there with his back to the window saying again to someone, "I really can't tell which one he is going to choose."

This time, Josh could tell there was another person as they provided a muffled response that he couldn't hear. Josh noticed that he moved away from the window and to the next room, which seemed to be at the very back of the house. As he walked away from the window, he began to say, "I am wondering what he is doing right now."

Josh wanted to get a better view of Tim to try and see who he was talking to, so he motioned again to Terra as a way to assure her he is continuing. Josh noticed that his next move was to go around the back of the house out of the sight of Terra. Yet the need to find out who Tim was talking to was more important in this moment. So, he moved again towards the back of the house. As he came around the corner, Tim was standing there at the back door staring at Josh and said to him slowly, "I wonder what he is doing right now."

Before Josh could run away, Tim grabbed him and dragged him into the house, locking the door behind him. He was a big, strong man that made it hard for Josh to escape his grip. Josh began to hear Tim say, "Josh, calm down, calm down, I am not going to hurt you."

Josh stopped squirming and managed to break away from the hold, looking Tim in the face, "How do you know my name?"

"I know all about you from my brother, but we won't talk about that for now," Tim said with his hands cautiously raised before his body. "I need to show you something."

Josh was confused and even scared as Tim moved towards a door, unsure of what was about to happen. Tim immediately opened the door and said, "Go in. Come on."
When Josh walked in the door, Tim closed the door behind him. He saw a room that had many different family pictures around the room. He could even hear a windchime playing outside the window. There was a peace in the room. Josh looked at the pictures and began to see a face of a young girl. Suddenly, from a chair in the corner by the window, a woman's voice spoke up, "Do you recognize her, Josh?" It was an older woman's voice that sounded as if she was emotional in his presence.
Josh looked at the chair and could see an older woman gazing out the window as if she was searching for something. She had long flowing gray hair. The frail curtains blocked her face as the wind blew in from the windows. Josh was staring and intrigued to know who this woman was.
"Josh, I know that you have so many questions right now," the woman said. "And I am here to try and help you have some answers. Look again at the pictures."
Josh looked again at the pictures and began to see a young girl that began to look more like his mother. The more he looked, the more he saw pictures of his mother growing up before his eyes. He kept searching through the pictures and eventually found a picture of his father and mother.
"How did you get these?" Who are you?" Josh asked. "How do you know your mother?"

"Josh put the clues together," The woman replied. "I am Ruth. I am your grandmother."

Josh stood there stunned as he realized he was talking with his grandmother for the first time. As tears began to roll down his cheeks, Ruth stood up and said, "Come here my boy." Josh ballooned towards his grandmother and fell in her arms. He dreamed for a moment that this was the way that his mother would have held him.

"Do you know why your mother and father named you Josh?" Ruth asked. "She said that she always knew that one day you would be someone of courage and strength, just like Joshua in the Bible. And just as Joshua faced many uncertain things, he always had courage to do the right thing no matter what the cost."

After Josh had a moment to collect his thoughts, he asked, "Why have I not been able to meet you? Where have you been my whole life?"

"That's a conversation for another day. What you need to know right now is that you are in serious danger along with all the Protectors and you need to have courage and strength," Ruth replied.

"Wait, you know about the Protectors?" Josh asked.

"Yes, I do, in fact I secretly have been one for a while, I just know it is too dangerous for me to see everyone at the Den," Ruth replied. "I hope my friend Thomas is doing well. But let's talk about some things," Ruth said as she motioned for Josh to sit in the seat next to her.

Josh sat down in the chair and could tell that she was emotional as she said, "ProTech and what is happening in Valley Hills is not what it seems."

"Oh, ProTech is no longer a problem, we got rid of Bale from the company," Josh said confidently.

Ruth reached out a grabbed Josh's hand and stared him in the eyes as she said, "Just because we don't see it, doesn't mean that it's not happening. There are things working behind the scenes that can hurt many people, if he is not stopped."

"Dek?" Josh asked. "No one has seen him for days or months. How do you know there is something happening?" Josh asked.

"For now, I need you to trust me and I need you to take a message back to Thomas and Cal," Ruth said.

"Okay," Josh said hesitantly.

"More to come. Things happening. Bale is back," Ruth said. "Can you do that for me?"

"Yes, will do." Josh the continued.

"So, if you are my grandmother, does that mean Tim is my…" Josh asked?

"Tim? Oh, you mean Duo. Your grandfather?" She began to laugh out loud. "No, he is not your grandfather." She smiled and continued, "Duo is…well, I believe you know his brother, Noah."

Josh's eyes opened wide as he asked, "Noah? You knew Noah? I didn't know ALLIs had brothers."

"Well, the reason that we call him Duo is that he was more like the second prototype of Noah. You do not remember him, since you were so young, but he was one of the test machines created by your mother that was tested. Dek didn't like how protective that he was of individuals, so he wanted to discard him. Deb thought it was best for him to come and watch over me. Along the way she made upgrades and now he helps me by getting things for me around the community, but yes, Tim is an ALLI," Ruth replied.

"So how does Tim know who I am?" Josh asked.

"Deborah often would put memories of Noah into Duo and she believes that is how he became so defensive for our family," Ruth said. "So as those memories have remained stored, so also have been things that Tim has been able to pick up from you in your connection with Noah. I can tell that you had a huge heart for Noah and I was terrified to hear of what happened to him at your last confrontation. In many ways I came to know you through him."

Josh then asked, "Ruth, did you write the code?"

"Yes!" Ruth replied.

"So, what does it all mean?" Josh asked.

"Well to different people, it will mean different things when they read it. Very few will know what all of it means, but I did that on purpose. But for now, you need to know that I need you to get the message back to the Protectors," Ruth said.

"Ruth…" Josh became solemn in a moment and asked, "Is my mother still alive?"

Ruth cracked a smile, "My boy, I want to tell you the whole story, but it is not my story to tell you. For now, trust the code, it will tell you what you need to know. What I can say is…"

Suddenly, the door opened and it was Tim.

"Mam, we have a situation that we need to move you to safety," Tim said.

"Wait, what can you say? What's going on?" Josh tried to get an answer from his grandmother.

Ruth's tone changed. "Were you followed in any way here?" Ruth asked Josh. "Is there anyone that knows that you are here?"
Josh hesitantly replied, "Just my friend Terra is outside watching for me. Oh man, it's been longer than 15 minutes and I told her that if I didn't come back, that she needed to call my dad for help."
"Go and get Terra and make sure that you do not come back to this house," Ruth said.
Josh began to move towards the front of the house to look out the window for Terra when Tim grabbed him and pulled him down to the floor.
"You have to watch for them," Tim said in a whisper as he put his finger over his mouth in a silencing motion.
"Who?" Josh whispered in reply.
"Human Allies," Tim whispered. As he said it, a dark black SUV slowly passed in front with the windows barely cracked and Josh could make out the face of Broderick, Bale's former security guard, as he drove by wearing his sunglasses.

Josh tried to catch a glance across the street to see if Terra was still there in the bushes. He could see her hiding out. He wondered how he could get her attention. He grabbed a mirror on a table and began to reflect the light to where she was.

She popped her head up just enough and Josh motioned for her to come to the side of the house. Just as he was about to motion again, suddenly the black SUV drove by again, and Tim grabbed Josh and pulled him to the ground.

"Mam, we really need to go," Tim said to Ruth. "I am getting word of a possible search at our house."

Josh wondered where Tim was getting his information from.

"There is more to tell you Josh," Ruth replied. "Another day and another time."

Josh looked back across the street and saw Terra, looking both ways to try and make her way to Ruth's house. When she reached the sidewalk at the front of the house, she gave Josh a thumbs up. Then, as if coming from nowhere, the black SUV showed up and two men jumped out and snatched Terra and to drag her to the back of the SUV. Josh could not believe what he was seeing. He yelled out, "Terra! Terra!"

Tim grabbed Josh and put his hand over her mouth to silence his yells. Josh began to cry out as he saw her continuing to kick.

"You have to be quiet," Tim began to whisper in his ear as he held him on the floor.

Josh continued to struggle against Tim, but Tim was too large to overcome.

"Josh, don't worry, we are going to get her back...." Tim said. Josh could see his face had some of the same features as those of Noah, "But for now, we have to get moving Ms. Ruth."

Ruth came out of the room where they had talked and said, "I am sorry to leave you in such short notice, but we have to go, I am, unfortunately, being watched."

"You will need to slip out the back," Tim said.

"When can I see you again? I have more questions," Josh asked.

"I will see you again," Ruth replied. "But for now, remember what I told you to pass along to Thomas, it is very important." She stopped for a moment and put her hand to Josh's face and said, "Your mother would be so proud to see the young man you have become."

"Now out the back son," Tim said. "And whatever you do, be careful."

Chapter 17

Contact Tracing

Josh was still in shock for a moment as to what he just experienced with Terra, Ruth, and Tim. He began to slowly ride his bicycle towards his home when he felt the presence of being watched. As a matter of precaution, when he reached the corner on the street, he stopped and decided to behind him. For a moment there was no one there and Josh thought it was all in his head. Then slowly, the black SUV turned down the same street where Josh came from and began to drive slowly. Josh thought for a moment if he should try and hide or if he should make a run for it. Suddenly, he heard a hissing sound immediately fly up in the sky. "Drones..." Josh said with a growl, "I hate drones,".

In a rush, Josh took off on his bicycle and darted across the street. He thought as long as I can ride across yards and through neighborhoods, it will be harder for them to track me. The SUV noticed Josh immediately and he could hear the tires spinning out to try and catch up to him. Josh saw an opening between two fences and rode between them. He looked back as he rode down the street and could hear the SUV's tires screeching to a halt to turn down the same street.

Just as he thought he was getting closer to being away, the hissing of the drone flew by his head. He knew that he wouldn't have a real chance to escape unless he could get rid of the drone. Josh looked up ahead and saw a house that had many large trees in the yard. Josh bared down and rode as fast as he could towards the house. It was rare to see a house with this number of large trees in Valley Hills but Josh was glad it was there. When Josh got to the house, he noticed that it had a large yard. So, he began to ride figure eights around the trees, knowing that he didn't have much time before the SUV would arrive to the same location. As Josh could hear the SUV getting closer and closer, he suddenly took off towards the back of the house to another street. The change of direction was too much for the drone and he could see that it got caught in the tree behind him.

As he looked back towards the trees, he pumped his fist in a moment of excitement thinking he had escaped, when suddenly was jolted and began to fly in the air over the handlebars of his bicycle. When he hit the ground, he rolled a couple of times, not knowing what happened. Still unsure of the cause, he tried to gather his thoughts as he knew he couldn't stay there long.

Suddenly, he heard a voice say, "you need to come with me." He recognized that voice. Still dazed he looked up slowly and could see it was Brittany there helping him to stand. She helped him to his feet and then went over to his bike, where the wheel was bent.

"Hurry, you have to come with me," Brittany said in a rush. She put his hands on the handlebars and said, "Here help me push your bike to these bushes." Josh and Brittany pushed the bike to a set of bushes beside a house, and almost immediately, Josh crashed against a fence to look over his body. Both his arms were scraped from the fall as well as his jeans were ripped.

"Is anything broken?" Brittany asked.

"Not that I can tell," Josh said through the pain.

"Wait, shh," Brittany said to Josh as she put her hand on his shoulder. Suddenly, the black SUV slowly drove by. Josh could hear Broderick in the car, "He got away. We will have to let the boss know. At least we have the girl."

As the car drove off, Brittany turned her attention back to Josh. "Are you sure you are ok?" Brittany asked.

"Yeah I think my bike is trashed, but yes, I will be ok," Josh said. "How did you find me here?"

Brittany replied, "Well, I was riding my bicycle and I saw the SUV going quickly through our streets. It made me stop and wonder what they were doing, but I didn't think anything about it, until I saw you riding down my street and could hear them speeding up to try and catch you. I thought you must be in trouble. So, I followed you to see what was happening. Then when you hit that pothole, and I could see you lying here needing help."

"Thanks," Josh replied almost trying to overcome the embarrassment of his wreck.

"By the way, are you in trouble? I am not harboring a fugitive or anything right?" Brittany playfully asked. "I mean it's not every day that you see a kid getting chased by a SUV like that."

"And it's not every day that you get chased by the HUMAN ALLIES," Josh said.

"Wait, that was the ALLIES?" Brittany asked. "Why are they after you? This is so major."

"Yeah and they took Terra," Josh said as he stood up and began to survey his bicycle wreckage.

"Wait, kidnapping, by the ALLIES? Are you sure?" Brittany replied.

"Yeah, I have to get to my friends and to home," Josh said as he began to pick up his bicycle.

"You have to tell the police. I mean, Terra is kidnapped. That's like illegal right?" Brittany said.

"Well, it's a little complicated right now. I'll have to explain it later," Josh began to push his bicycle and it was not moving well.

"Hey why don't you let my mom give you a ride home? We live just two streets over," Brittany offered.

"Oh, I will be fine," Josh said as he tried to push his bicycle again and this time the wheel fell completely off. Realizing it was a lost cause he replied, "Ok, but you can't say anything about Terra, just please say that you helped me after my bicycle wreck."

--

When Josh and Brittany arrived at her house, she said, "Hey just wait here. My mom probably doesn't want you coming into the house with all the blood and stuff."

"No problem," Josh said as he crashed on the steps in the garage still in pain from the wreck.

He looked at the vehicles in the garage and they were really nice. He noticed that there were things in the garage that both a girl and a boy could play with. The stickers on the cars were for ProTech employees but they looked different from normal stickers.

Brittany could hear muddled voices inside the house sounding like concern and then quieter, when suddenly Brittany emerged from the house and said, "We are good to go. Just sit there in the back seat. Mom also asked if you could sit on these towels."

As Josh slipped into the backseat of the car, he noticed the pristine condition of the car and was even cautious about touching anything in the car, especially realizing that he was still bloody from the wreck. As he sat down he could hear Brittany's mother emerge from the house. Not paying attention to what was going on and still in pain from the accident, Josh put his head in his hands.

"So where are we going?" the voice said.

Josh slowly began to rattle off Abby and Ty's address, "4 Privet…" but then stopped when he looked up and saw it was Lucinda Bellliston, the CEO of Protech.

"Say that again. I didn't catch the whole address," Lucinda said.

In a moment of realizing that he didn't want to reveal Ty and Abby's address, he quickly shifted and said, "100 Security Ave."

"Oh, that's different from what you began to say?" Lucinda asked.

He quickly replied, "Sorry, I must still be dazed from the accident."

The atmosphere in the vehicle quickly changed as Josh realized that he was sitting with someone that was open to the removal of the Protectors. Yet he was confused about how Brittany was her daughter and was so nice. He noticed how Lucinda had small pictures of what seemed to be Brittany and another child, whose profile was hidden behind Brittany's picture.

"Brittany tells me how you have really been a good to friend to her in the school," Lucinda said.

"Mom, you are embarrassing me," Brittany said as she blushed.

"Oh, glad to help," Josh said with a straight a face that he could. He noticed how Lucinda often would look at him in the rear-view mirror.

"I bet your parents are going to be surprised to hear what happened to you. Now who are they again?" Lucinda asked.

"Well…" Josh was looking for a way to get out of having to answer the question.

Brittany then began to yell out, "Mom, look, Carrie's Boutique is ready to release their new line up of clothes!"

Josh was relieved to hear the change of subject and yet he looked up and could see Lucinda looking at him through the rear view mirror.

"That seems like a pretty big wreck you had. Where were you going?" Lucinda asked.

"Mom, I already told you, Josh rides his bicycle everywhere and he hit one of those potholes," Brittany said.

"Well, I am glad that my little B was there to help you," Lucinda said.

"Me too, she's a lifesaver!" Josh replied.

"Here we are, 100 Security Avenue, " Lucinda said. "and you don't see that every day."

Before everyone's eyes was a lime green van, plastered with the words:

ADVENTURES WITH BARRY

Next to the words was a picture of Barry, with no shirt on, wearing a cowboy hat, shorts, and sunglasses, and underneath the picture was his contact information.

"So, this is your home?" Lucinda asked with an interrogating tone.

"Well, my parents are not home right now, and this is where I come when they aren't there," Josh said.

About that time, Barry came out of the house wearing a cut off white shirt, his cowboy hat, shorts, and cowboy boots, almost identical to the picture on the van. He grabbed the water hose lying in the yard and began to spray off his van.

"So, you are going to be ok?" Brittany said.

"Yes, and thank you again for the ride and taking care of me," Josh said. "I guess I will see you tomorrow at school."

"Yes, see you later," Brittany replied.

"Take care, Josh," Lucinda added. "See you real soon," as she stared at Josh getting out of the vehicle.

As soon as Josh got out of the car, Barry began to shout, "What is up my bro? Who's the ladies? Did you give them my email address?"

Josh replied, "What's up Barry? Just some people that gave me a ride home. I had a major wreck on my bike."

"Dude, that is awesome," Barry replied, "Did you get it on video?"

"No man, sorry I missed it. Hey is Bub here?" Josh asked.

"Yeah man, he's inside with Yash man." Barry then paused and grabbed Josh's arm, "Are you ok, dude?"

Josh paused for a moment and then said, "Barry, I'm trying to figure it out."

"Hey, you know that I have learned," Barry said. "The times that I try to figure it out on my own, are when I mess it all up. The biggest adventure you can have is not when you try to set your own course, but when you trust the road that God is taking you down." Josh leaned back from Barry as It caught him off guard for Barry to have shared something so deep.

"Where did that come from?" Josh replied sarcastically.

"Dude I am living out the greatest adventure with the Lord. Not sure how or why things happen the way that they do, but it's just where He takes me," Barry said. "Plus, you get to meet pretty girls along the way…just don't tell Jeanine, you know what I'm saying."

There was the old Barry everyone knew. "I'm sure Twinkie is inside eating," Barry said. "By the way, I want my radio name to be Bond, Barry Bond. Deal?"

"No problem, you know that's an old baseball player, right?" Josh replied as he walked away and Barry turned on some heavy metal music.

"Yeah, it's cool. We are good." Barry yelled as Josh walked away. Josh looked back at Barry and could hear him shouting over the music, "It's Christian heavy metal! I love it!"

Josh came in the front door and could hear the sounds of video games playing upstairs. He walked slowly up the stairs and found Bub and Yashi sitting in his room with their headphones on, oblivious to the world.

"Bub...Bub...BUB!!" Josh said to get Bub's attention. "Oh, hey man, I have been trying to get in contact with you about playing. You want something to eat?"

"No," Josh said as he walked over and turned off the game. "Terra has been kidnapped."

"Whatever...you are playing a joke on me..." Bub said as he chuckled.

"No! I am serious. She has been kidnapped by the Human Allies," Josh replied.

"We have to call the police. We have to let them know what is going on," Yashi said, "What happened?"

"Terra and I were following the janitor..." Josh then recounted all the details that he could remember, even stating how Brittany was Lucinda's daughter.

They were both in shock over everything he heard and said. "So, we can't really go to the police because it may reveal how we are all Protectors. We need to get to Ezzie."

"Yeah, that's true," Josh said.

Just as they were about to form their plan, Josh's phone began to ring, it was Aunt Abby. Josh knew that if he missed this call that it would be major trouble again. So, he stepped out into the hallway and answered to try and give at least a quick response. "Aunt Abby, I am fine, I can't really talk right now, I am at Bub's."

"Josh...JOSH..." Abby replied with a tone in her voice that Josh had never heard before. "It's your dad."

"What about my dad?" Josh asked.

"He's missing, I need you to come home to make sure that you are safe," Abby said.

"What? How?" As the questions raced through Josh's mind.

"Just come home and let's figure it out from here," Abby said.

"Ok bye," Josh shocked by the news stepped back into Bub's room.

"What happened? You don't look so well?" Yashi asked.

"My dad is missing and I have to go home," Josh replied.

"First, Terra gets kidnapped and now your dad is missing as well," Bub said, "We have to get you out of here. Let's see if Barry can give you a ride home."

Josh thought for a moment, "Brittany's mom was acting weird in the car and I'm scared to just take off, since I had them to drop me off here. We could get trailed or even have them try to come and get my family."

At that moment, Josh could hear outside the sound of an engine coming down the street. He looked and slowly rolling by the house was the black SUV, the same as before. As they passed by, Josh Yashi, and Bub ducked down their heads.

"What we need is a distraction to get you out of here," Bub said.

Barry then bust into the room and said, "What you need is Adventures with Barry! Sorry little bros, heard all the heavy stuff while out in the hallway. You are in a pinch and I am here to get you unpinched. So, let's do it!" As Barry did a karate kick in the air.

"Here give me your jacket," Bub said.

"My jacket is not going to fit you..." Josh replied.

"I know that, but the people watching the house don't know that" Bub said, "Let me and Barry take off and then you and Yashi can slip out the back."

"I'll need to borrow your bike, since mine is trashed," Josh said.

"No problem take care of her, we have been through a lot," Bub replied with a sentimental tone.

Barry and Bub went out of the house and got in Barry's van. Barry could see where the SUV was and started to make his way towards the vehicle. He rolled down the window and said something to the driver and then immediately started to speed off. The SUV did a U-turn in the street and took off after Barry. The plan was actually working.

Josh and Yashi began to take off on their bicycles towards his house. They were cautious at each intersection and even cut through some backyards to make it to the house.

Chapter 18

Profile Update

When Josh and Yashi came in the house, they were greeted at the door by Ty and Abby with huge hugs, but Josh still feeling the effects of his bike wreck moaned in pain. Abby ushered Josh into the kitchen to begin to tend to his wounds, and he noticed that Ezzie and Ty were there.

"Josh, what happened?" Ty asked.

"I had a bike wreck trying to escape," Josh said.

"Escape from whom?" Ty asked.

"The Human Allies," Josh said. "I was trying to escape from them. Somehow they had followed me to grandmother's house."

"You met Ruth?" Thomas asked.

"Yes and she wanted me to pass along a message to you all," Josh said, "More to come. Things happening. Bale is back."

"And that is all she said?" Ezzie asked.

"Yes well we talked about more stuff but that's not the worst of it all," Josh said as he hung his head. "Terra has been kidnapped!" Josh said.

"Terra, oh no!" Abby gasped as she put her hand over her mouth, "I'll call her parents to let her know."

"That is fine but they can't call the police," Josh said.

"Why? Do you know who did this?" Ty asked.

"Yes, it was the Human Allies," Josh said.

'Are you sure it was the Allies?" Ezzie asked.

"Yes, it was Broderick and I heard him say that they were going to talk with their boss," Josh replied.

Ty looked at Thomas and asked, "What does it mean? What Ruth said?"

Thomas looked at Josh and asked, "You are sure that is all she said?"

"Yes sir," Josh replied.

"Does this mean that Dek Bale is back?" Abby asked. "Is that why Cal is missing?"

"I'm not sure, I need to think and pray," Thomas said.

"What happened to my dad?" Josh asked.

Ezzie replied, "We aren't sure, all we know is that your dad was supposed to make contact with some Protectors in the capital of Northern California. He is trying to make contact with some of the legislators there to help stop ProTech being so powerful and in control of so many things in our world. He was supposed to have returned this afternoon, but no one has heard from him since he left."

"We have to go look for him," Josh replied.

"I know exactly where they are…all of them," the voice came from the front door and when everyone looked, it was Ruth standing in the doorway.

"Ruth!" Thomas exclaimed as he rushed over to greet her. She was apparently out of breath and in distress.

"I need to sit down. Can someone give me some water?" Ruth said between breaths. "They have taken Duo as well when they tried to get me. Luckily, I was able to escape. I thought this would be the best place to get the help that I need.

"How did you escape?" Abby asked.

"Duo was so brave and he was able to fend off the Broderick and his men just long enough for me to get away. I drove around to make sure that I was not being followed and I decided to come here," Ruth said between breaths. "I believe it is time for us all to have a conversation."

Everyone sat in silence as they focused in on Ruth.

She began, "Josh, Dek Bale is more than you think that he is. When I was giving birth to your mother, I was so excited to have her come into the world. But even more than that, I was surprised when your uncle, Dek was born. I tried to encourage them to play sports and do activities outside, but I could see that their interest was in computers. And they were great at it as you all know. When I started to show signs of aging, Deborah originally wanted to use AI to create a way to care for me while she was working for ProTech. Therefore, she began to prototype of what we all know to be Noah and eventually Duo. Dek, though had different plans. Plans for domination and the abuse of technology. With his desire for more, came his desire for more power. Yet they could begin to see the difference in ideas becoming more and more different.

When the night happened of your mother's wreck, the night of your birth, it was a tragedy and there were things happening in that moment that none of us could stop. No one could stop Dek from his plans.

You see when your mother had her wreck she went into a coma for twelve years."

Josh stopped her and said, "That means that my mother is…"

"Yes!" Ruth replied, "You mother is alive, but she is in great danger. Dek has kept her hidden in a secret house off River's Edge Road and he had me to watch over her each day."

"River's Edge Road has been shut down for years," Ty said.

"Twelve years in fact," Ruth replied. "It's a house there that he had built after the wreck. With your mother being in her coma, I knew that if I ever left her side, Dek would do something to Deborah to prevent her from receiving the care she needed. Then a year ago, your mother suddenly came out of the coma. It was around the same time that you infiltrated ProTech and he went to prison for a short period of time. I slowly started to help her recover with physical therapy and to help her get strength back. About nine months ago, Dek came to her and said that she could in no way let her presence be known and that if she ever did, he would hurt you and Cal. So, she has been under heavy security watch for the last year at Dek's secret house, keeping her being alive a secret.

Six months ago, we made a plan to escape but unfortunately, only I was able to escape. However, I was able to find Duo through an old connection that I had at ProTech, I believe you know him as James Newton. When I came back, I knew that I needed to begin to reach out to you and the other Protectors. That is why I used the code,

"40 days are over. 40 nights are not. The Rose has bloomed, remember where one was not, one is now. Two know where one is but not one."

Ruth began to explain,
"'40 days are over. 40 nights are not.' Dek is going to continue to use the blackouts as long as he possibly can until his work is finished.
'The Rose has bloomed' that is a reference to your mother. As we both know that her favorite flower was the rose, in fact I believe you still wear her cross with the rose on it.
'Remember where one was not, one is now.' She has come back and is ready.
Abby then interjected, "How exciting that this all is! To think that Deborah is alive!"
Ruth looked at everyone with a somber tone, "I need to tell you that the situation is worse than it has ever been. Dek is out of control and I believe the days that are coming are far worse. He has found a new way to use AI and it involves both the use of AL-LI's as well as mind control in humans. The blackouts are coming from him needing power for his work at his secret house. But he has a plan to use the celebration as a way to announce him comeback and to reveal the plans for his takeover using microchips. The microchips will be implanted in each person and then…"
"The AI will take over their minds to have them to do whatever Dek wants…" Ezzie said.
"If he can take over the minds, he can control the actions. He is basically turning everyone into ALLI's," Thomas said.

"We have to get into that house and stop Bale," Thomas said.

"Ruth, is there a time that Bale works on his experiments more than others?" Abby asked.

"The next blackouts will be for three hours on Wednesday nights," Yashi said to everyone's surprise. "What? My dad has it calculated to the minute. They start at 7PM."

"Ok so we have to try and get there by tomorrow night," Ty said.

"We need a layout of the facility as much as possible," Thomas said. "Do you remember how everything worked there Ruth?"

"Yes," Ruth said, "I will try to remember as much as I can but I will tell you that the house has a vulnerability. It was how I was able to escape."

"What is it?" Abby asked.

"Not as much what, as it is who?" Ruth replied. "Does the name Ryan Ahabin ring any bells?"

"Wait a second," Ezzie said. "You don't mean, Ryan Ahabin, Jezzie Ahabin's brother? I'm not sure about this…"

"He snuck me out by way of a food delivery service truck. He was my only way to get out of there. He is a good man and I trust him," Ruth replied. "And I am sure that if he the way out, he can be the way back in. In fact, I found Duo because Jezzie told him to tell me to find James."

"What if this is all a big plan to get Josh to go there? We remember him saying beforehand that all he wanted to do was to remove the obstacles in the way," Abby asked.

"It's a big risk, but it's our only hope right now," Thomas said. "Ruth, can you reach out to Ryan to let him know that we need to get in?"

"Yes. What do we need?" Ruth asked.

"We will need uniforms from Ryan's company to make it look like we are employees and able to walk around the facility," Thomas said.

"Right, if we can get inside the walls then we can find Deborah and the others and help them to escape," Ty chimed in.

"Yeah, but we are also going to need a distraction to draw people away from where they are hiding," Abby said.

"I have an idea," Bub said.

Everyone began to look amused not sure what he was going to say.

"Ok what is it Bub?" Ty said casually.

"Use the HUMAN ALLIES," Bub said.

"Aren't those the guys that hate the Protectors and are trying to get us?" Thomas chimed in.

"Yeah, so if we say that Bale's house is the place for the blackouts, they aren't going to know that it is Bale's place. Also, we can say that the Protectors will be there," Bub replied.

"Caden will then be forced to host a protest at Bale's house," Yashi said.

"So how can we get word to them?" Abby asked.

"I'll take care of that," Bub said.

"Ok what can we do?" Josh asked.

"Josh it is too dangerous for you to be there," Ty said, "You will need to stay here with Abby, Ruth, Desirae, and Bradley. It is just too risky and I do not want to put you into a dangerous place like last time."

"No, no, no, I can't," Josh said, "I am old enough, I know what risks are involved, I have to save my mom, dad, Terra, and Duo."

"It's just too risky!" Abby said. "We will need to help provide some guidance to them while they are moving around the facility." She then looked at Ezzie, "What would we need to hack into their system?"

"I can make it happen," Ezzie said.

As the others continued to make their plans, Josh stepped away from the group out on the front porch with Yashi.

"I feel like I have to be involved. I can't just stand by and watch," Josh said.

"What can we do though?" Yashi said. "You heard them that this is going to be dealing with security and stuff."

"I'm not sure, but I have to do something," Josh said.

Chapter 19

The Escape Button

It was around 6:30 p.m. when Ryan, Ty, Thomas, and Ezzie began to head towards Bale's house. Thomas sat in the front seat of the truck with Ryan as they arrived at the secret house off River Edge Road, while Ty and Ezzie stayed in the back of the truck hidden. When they pulled up to the entrance of the house, Ryan rolled down the window to show them ID's and the guards let them in.

They drove through a large gate and veered towards the access to the kitchen. The house has a large metal fence surrounding it with a spacious courtyard beside it filled with different large statues and decorations and a fountain sitting close to the house. Thomas notices how the guards are not armed with guns, but they do have tasers on them.

When Ryan pulled up to the kitchen, he reached down and disconnected some wires underneath the dash. This way his battery and starter were disconnected and it would look like he had a bad battery and could not move the vehicle.

Ty and Thomas wore their uniforms as they began to roll boxes of fake food around the building. Suddenly, it was 7 p.m. and the lights all went out in the house and across Valley Hills. Ty and Thomas took off their uniform shirts and put them in the box wearing only black shirts to move around in the dark easier. They also had some night vision goggles and flashlights that helped them to move around. Ezzie had placed tracers on them and he was able to get a set of schematics of the building. They set up the food service truck where Ezzie could stay in the truck to access the security system while Ty and Thomas went around the grounds looking for everyone.

Back at the Den, everyone was able to see the security camera feed coming through. This allowed for Ruth to be able to relay information by radio to Ty, Thomas, as they navigated through the different rooms. "Stop! That's the door. Deborah should be in there." Ruth said with confidence. Ty stood outside while Thomas opened the door, looked in the room, and saw that no one was in there. He radioed back, "She is not in here Ruth. Any more ideas."

"She should be in there." Ruth said. "Unless it is…"

"What?" Thomas said.

"A trap! You need to get out of there," Ruth said.

Immediately, Ty and Thomas were swarmed with guards and taken into custody.

"We have to help them," Josh said. "Aunt Abby, we have to go."

Josh looked at Abby and she nodded in affirmation to Josh.

Josh looked at Bub and said, "You know who we need."

"It's Barry time!" Bub replied.

Bub immediately got on the radio that was at the Den and began to call out, "Bond, Barry Bond, come in."

"Isn't that a baseball player?" Abby asked.

"Yes, we tried to explain to him but he doesn't care," Bub said. "Repeat Bond, Barry Bond, you are needed at the Den,"

There was a brief moment of pause on the radio when the silence was broken through with "Twinkie, Bond is on the way."

It didn't take long before the sound of heavy metal music began to rattle through the Den. Abby grasped Josh by his face and said, "Be careful."

"I am going as well," Ruth said. "If there is someone that can help Josh, it is me."

Abby got on the radio, "Ezzie are you still there?"

"Yeah, I'm here, not sure what is going on except Ty and Thomas are caught," Ezzie responded.

"Don't worry, the Protectors are coming," Abby said.

--

Barry pulled the van just down the road from the house. He let Josh, Bub, Yashi, and Ruth out.

"Barry, keep an eye out for us. When you see us flashing the lights at you, pull up to the gate and we will be ready to go," Josh said.

"You got it dude, Full House reference," Barry said.

Josh, Bub, Yashi, and Ruth began to walk through the woods to outside the gate of the house. The lights were still out at the house but the sound of generators were in the background to run large lights that were on top of the corners of the house to shine around the perimeter.

Josh and the friends were able to see the front gate. It was around 7:30PM and suddenly the noise of cars began to make its way towards the house. There seemed to be hundreds of people showing up. The HUMAN ALLIES came through and they were starting to stage a protest outside the walls demanding the Protectors to turn on the power. When Josh and the others saw that the guards were all focusing their attention and lights to the protestors at the front gate, Josh and the others all moved towards the side of the fence. Ruth said, "There is a small gate just right here around the corner that sometimes is left unlocked." When they arrived at the small gate, Ruth was able to jiggle the handle and then it popped open and they were able to slip into the courtyard unnoticed.

Josh came on the radio and whispered, "Bond, we are in the courtyard."

As Josh and the others began to move towards the back door, suddenly a light began to flash across the courtyard. It froze everyone to jump behind statues and even act like they were a part of the decorations. Bub one time even froze against the side of a statue where his stomach seemed to look like it was a part of the statue.

Ruth motioned for the group to keep moving forward. They reached the back door of the house and they were able to slip into the house. Bub said, "For a house that has all this security, they like to leave their doors unlocked." As he said this, they could hear that there was someone about to enter into the room where they were, so they all hid in different spots.

As they hid, the voices became clearer and Josh recognized them as being Dek Bale, Lucinda Belliston, and Broderick.

"Lucinda, can you tell me why your son is at my front door protesting me?" Dek said angrily.

"It must be the Protectors; they must have sent them here," Lucinda said.

Lucinda turned to Broderick and said. "Let Caden know that they need to leave."

Dek then spoke up again, "I want all the Protectors found before tomorrow night's announcement. If we have to put them all in the cooler, we will. I say that we start to interrogate the ones that we have. I think we can begin with the youngest one, Terra, she should be able to get us the information that we need. Use whatever means necessary"

"Dek, I need to know that whether we find them or not, is this going to go off without a any problems tomorrow night? We have a lot riding on this and we need to get these contracts," Lucinda chimed in.

Rather than answering her question, Dek asked Broderick, "Broderick, are we sure that this is going to be ok?"

"Yes sir," Broderick said confidently.

Dek left the room and Lucinda pulled Broderick back into the room before they left. "Broderick, the only way that this is going to happen is if Dek is not a part of ProTech moving forward. Remember the plan, that once we have the technology in hand, then Dek is out. And I think we both know what out means."

"Yes mam," Broderick said as he lifted up a syringe.

They left the room. When it seemed that they were away, Josh popped his head up and whispered, "Hey is everyone ok? I wish I had that on a recording."

"Hey Josh, I don't know if this is a good time to say this, but I used my SLUG while they were talking. I actually think it worked this time," Bub said with excitement.

Before Josh could say anything in response, they heard the doors beginning to move open and they all knelt back down. It was two people sneaking through the room in the dark with a flashlight. Josh looked for a moment to see who they were and he then whispered, "Ezzie, is that you?"

Ezzie and Ryan turned around immediately and put their flashlight right on Josh's face. "Josh, I'm glad to see that you are okay? We have been sneaking around the house looking for everyone."

Josh replied, "We just heard all the plans by Dek and they have everyone in what they call the cooler."

"I know where it is, follow me," Ruth said.

"Wait do all of us need to go?" Ryan asked. "Should some of us be lookouts or something in case it all goes bad."

"Good idea," Ezzie replied. "Ryan, you take Bub and Yashi back with you to the truck. Be a watch out for us and if you hear or see anything, use the radios. Josh, Ruth, and I will go to the cooler."

As Ryan, Bub, and Yashi began to leave, Bub asked, "So what kind of truck do you have?"

"it's a food truck," Ryan replied.

A smile came across Bub's face when he heard that in the truck was food.

--

When the others left, Josh turned to Ezzie. "Ezzie, we have a problem."

"What is it Josh?" Ezzie asked.

"Dek is not only the villain but also the victim. He thinks that he is making a discovery to take back over ProTech, but Lucinda Belliston has plans to remove Dek from the equation that he doesn't know about. We are going to have to stop both of them at the same time, while saving everyone," Josh said.

As they navigated through the hallways, they were able to find the place that Ruth knew as the cooler. She motioned towards the door and watched them enter.

When Josh moved into the room, it was still dark and their flashlights were able to make out a hallway filled with small rooms with little windows for each one. There was an eerie coldness to the room. They went to the first room and looked in there and no one was in there. Then they went to the next room and could see Terra sitting in there. Josh knocked on the window and she looked up and smiled.

She motioned towards a desk sitting in the corner of the hallway. Ezzie went there and began to go through the drawers. He found a set of keys. They opened the door to let Terra out. Ruth looked her over and asked if she was ok. In the next room was Cal, Ty, and Thomas. As they opened the door, Thomas said, "Josh, I'm sorry that I ever doubted you. They have taken your mother and Duo to Bale's room."

Josh embraced his father and said, "I'm glad you are ok dad." Josh could tell he was weak.

Josh looked at Ruth, "Where is Bale's room?"

"It's in a high secure area that I was never allowed to go close to," Ruth replied.

Suddenly a long blaring alarm started to sound everywhere. Ruth said, "That is the alarm that the power is about to come back on. I think I know how to draw them all out. Follow me."

Everyone followed Ruth to the courtyard area. She told everyone to hide.

When the lights came back on all over the facility, Ruth was standing alone in the middle of the courtyard. All of security saw her standing there and pointed all their lights to her. The rest of the Protectors hid in the shadows.

"DEK…" Ruth began to shout aloud. "DEK BALE!"

Broderick came out to the courtyard followed by Lucinda. "Ruth, I am not sure what you are hoping to accomplish here."

"It's time for me to talk to my son, Broderick," Ruth replied.

"You know that's not going to happen Ruth," Broderick said.

"Oh yes, it is! Either he comes here or I will share your plan Broderick," Ruth said.

Suddenly Bale's entered the courtyard followed by Deborah and Duo being escorted by guards. "Well…mother deary is here!" Bale announced. "In fact, the whole family is here, Cal, Deborah, Josh, well maybe not Josh…Let's just have a family reunion."

"Dek the show is over. I am telling you as your mother, you can stop this. There are things happening behind the scenes that are going to hurt you," Ruth said.

"Ruth, mother, you always wanted to stop progress," Bale said. "When we tried to make the world a safer place with our ALLIs, it was you and Deborah that always tried to take the moral high ground. But here is the thing, artificial intelligence is replacing intelligence. From this day forward, Dek Bale is making his own morality. And here it is," Dek held up his hand with a piece of paper. "Here is the patent for the microchips that I created that are forever going to form the way we live in this world for generations to come."

"Dek, you are so talented," Ruth replied. "Just know that you are not the only one wanting to have that piece of paper, is it Lucinda?"

Dek began to look confused, "What's she talking about Lucinda?"

"I have no idea, Dek, she is crazy. All she wants is that piece of paper for herself," Lucinda replied.

Josh could hear Bub coming through on the radio, "Noah…Soul Man…this is Twinkie. Is everything ok?"

Josh whispered, "Bub, we can't talk right now. Ruth is talking with Dek and Lucinda both right now in front of everyone."

"Man, I wish I could see everything through Noah's eyes in this moment," Bub said.

"That's it," Josh said. "Bub, do you know if the SLUG worked?"

"I mean I can try and see if it did or not," Bub replied.

"You have to try it and see if it does. Use Ezzie's equipment in the back of the truck," Josh said.

Bub went to the back and found a piece of audio equipment connected to the radios. He put a cord from the speaker to the piece of gum. Then he said, "let's see if this works."

He clicked a button and told Josh, "Put me on the radio. Turn it up loud."

Immediately, Josh and Yashi both stepped forward from hiding and began to turn on and off their flashlights while they turned up their radio. Suddenly the audio of the conversation of Lucinda and Broderick began to ring out across the courtyard. The volume was such that even the protesters outside the gate could hear what was being said.

"*Broderick, the only way that this is going to happen is if Dek is not a part of ProTech moving forward. Remember the plan, that once we have the technology in hand, then Dek is out. And I think we both know what out means. "Yes mam."*
The audio was then repeated,
"*Broderick, the only way that this is going to happen is if Dek is not a part of ProTech moving forward. Remember the plan, that once we have the technology in hand, then Dek is out. And I think we both know what out means. "Yes mam."*

Then Bub's voice came through the radio, "The SLUG works! I knew it, the SLUG works! Twinkie is awes…."
Josh turned off the radio, "Tell them whose voice that is Lucinda."
Lucinda began to laugh out loud, "Dek these people are crazy. Let's get this over with."
"Wait a second," Dek said, "You are planning to get rid of me? You want all of ProTech for yourself."
"Mom? Was that you?" Lucinda turned to see Caden from the HUMAN ALLIES looking at his mother in shock.
"Son, this is all made up. It is the Protectors. They are the evil ones," Lucinda tried to reply.
"No mom, it was you!" Another voice came from behind Caden. It was Brittany. "I didn't believe it when Josh said that the HUMAN ALLIES were trying to kidnap him. But now it makes sense that you were using the ALLIES to control all of us and to remove the Protectors. Josh, I am sorry that this happened."
Lucinda replied sternly, "You have no idea what I have sacrificed to get us here to this point. We are at the point of becoming the world's most powerful people, and you want to throw it all away?"

"Enough games…" Immediately, Broderick grabbed Ruth and held the syringe to her throat. "Bale this was originally made for you, but I will be glad to use this on your mother. Just hand over the paper to Lucinda."

"Woah…woah…everyone chill out," Bale said.

Lucinda spoke up, "Oh please, you are finished Bale. You may have the brains but you don't have the guts to be a real person of power. You will always have your weakness and now we know how to expose it, every time. Just hand over the paper."

About that time, the sound of heavy metal music began to get louder and closer. Everyone's attention turned towards the gate as they started to look to see the source of the sound through the darkness. Then suddenly, the lights from the van turned on and it crashed into the gates sliding into the courtyard. Barry jumped on to the roof of the van with his paintball gun and yelled, "It's time for Adventures with Barry, Rambo style!" Barry then started to shoot off a series of paintballs at the security guards.

The distraction was enough for Ruth to break from Broderick's grasp and she began to run towards the other Protectors. Thomas reached out his hands for her to help protect her from everything happening as they all started to move towards the van. Deborah and Duo were also able to break free from the security guards during Barry's entrance and ran to Cal to hide away behind some of the statues.

Josh pulled Duo aside and said, "Duo, it is time for protection mode."

"What do you mean?" Duo said confused.

"Duo, I need you to access Noah's memories, it's time for protection mode," Josh said.

Duo's eyes flashed for a moment. Josh then saw Duo's eyes come back to light. "Duo, are you there?" Josh said.

"It's not Duo, it's Noah and it's time to get you home," The demeanor on Duo's face changed. He held up two fingers to Josh, and Josh connected his fingers to his.

Duo began going after the different security guards that were trying to impede the Protectors from escaping. It was like watching a live action fight scene being played out.

Then, the food service truck came around the corner and the rear door slid up. Bub was standing there with food in his hand and yelled out, "Twinkie to the rescue! Come on everyone, in the truck!"

While Ruth and Thomas were running to the truck, Broderick grabbed Thomas' shoulders to turn him around and try to inject the syringe of poison. At that moment, Ruth stepped in front of Thomas and Broderick plunged the syringe into her chest. Thomas and Ruth were both shocked at what happened in that moment. Duo's attention immediately focused on Ruth. He rushed over and immediately knocked out Broderick. He then picked up Ruth and carried her to the truck. Her body lied there almost lifeless and her breath was becoming less and less.

Deborah rushed to her side, "Mom…mom, we can get you to the hospital."

"Oh honey, it's too far. But I have enjoyed my fun for today," Ruth replied.

Bale noticed what happened to his mother, dropped the paper in his hand, and rushed over to the other side of his mother. "Mom, I take back all those things that I said, please don't leave me."

"Oh, my two special children. Here together at last," Ruth said. "My race is over children. Now it's time to run your race. Where's Josh?" Josh knelt down beside his grandmother as she said, "You are so strong and courageous."

Josh began to look around and yell, "Someone do something. We have to do something now."

"Josh...Josh!" Ruth got his attention, "I told you that I am proud of the man that you have become. My time has come. The code is not finished..." And in that moment, she breathed her last.

Josh stood in shock of what just happened. His mother grabbed Josh as tight as she could and held him for the first time. It was the embrace that Josh longed for from his mother and yet it was happening at one of the worst moments in his life.

Deborah began to pull Josh towards the food truck to get in, but something caught his eye. It was the paper that Bale held in his hand that started to blow away. As he saw it moving along the ground, suddenly it was stopped as Lucinda put her foot on the paper and picked it up. "I have it!" as she let out a harrowing laugh.

Josh for a moment, let go of his mother's grip and knew that the only way to stop Lucinda was to get that piece of paper. Josh took off to chase after Lucinda. While Deborah was sitting in the truck beside her mother, she yelled for Josh.

Cal noticed what was happening and he took off after Josh.

She immediately ran back into the house. Josh was able to follow her up to the second floor that was Bale's office. When she ran into the office, she called her helicopter to come and pick her up. Josh rushed into the office, "It's over Lucinda."

His voice startled her and she started looking through Bale's desk for anything that could be used as a weapon. She opened the middle drawer and she found a gun and immediately pointed it towards Josh. "You are going to let me out of this house right now. It's not over. You are over. The Protectors are over. Move out of the way."

Then, Cal came rushing into the room. Lucinda began to point the gun at both Josh and Cal. "Stay where you are! Don't come one step closer or I'll shoot! I am leaving here!"

About that time, one more set of footsteps came into the room. It was Brittany.

Lucinda began to scream at Brittany, "B get out of here now! You don't need to see this!"

"Mom...MOM!" Brittany said to get her attention, "It's over." As she said the words, she moved in front of Josh and Cal. I am not going to let you hurt anyone else."

Tears began to roll down Lucinda's face. "Honey, you need to move. These people are going to tear us apart. We will never be the same."

"Mom, these are my friends. They are here to protect us not hurt us," Brittany replied.

Lucinda lowered the gun and motioned for Brittany to come to her in an embrace.

The sound of the helicopter started to rattle the windows. Lucinda realized that this was her last effort, "I'm sorry honey, mommy has to win." She then threw Brittany down to the ground and raised the gun to shoot. When she shot, she missed them and busted a window.

Without thinking, Cal rushed towards Lucinda and began to have a struggle with her. He was able to knock the gun out of her hand and she dropped the piece of paper in the process. Lucinda then kicked Cal and he fell to the ground.

Josh reached down and picked up the paper on the ground. Lucinda rushed towards him and they broke through the window together. Cal rushed over to the window to find both Josh dangling out the window holding on with Lucinda beside him. Cal grabbed Josh and helped him back in the room. While he was climbing back in, he dropped the piece of paper by the window. As Cal reached back to help Lucinda, she reached for the piece of paper. Yet when she grabbed it, she lost her grip and fell.

Suddenly, there was a large splash as she landed in the large fountain below. Everyone rushed over to see what happened. She was lying on her back and Ty jumped in to help her. She looked back and the paper was destroyed in the water and she began to cry.

The sounds of the action were immediately pierced by the sounds of sirens. It was the police and they all began to rush to the scene. The security guards all began to hold their hands up in surrender.

Lucinda began to scream and point to the Protectors, "Arrest them. Arrest them all!"

The police chief said, "You heard her men, "Arrest them."

Lucinda began to laugh as she pointed at the Protectors.

"Not them," The chief ordered. "Them!" He pointed to Lucinda and Broderick and said, "Broderick, you are under arrest for the murder of Ruth Bale…and Lucinda Belliston, you are under arrest for conspiracy to murder. I'm sure your investors will love to hear about this. But in case they don't hear it, they can watch it."

The chief turned towards the Protectors, "Luckily, some of our officers are fans of Adventures with Barry. Barry, I have to say this was one of your finest videos."

Barry stood at attention and saluted the chief, "Always read to serve, captain."

"I'm the chief," the chief replied.

"Whatever, sir," Barry snapped.

"I believe the audio as well will be great evidence in court," The chief said.

"Thanks sir," Bub said as he moved forward and saluted.

'SLUG's, you may be on to something there!" The chief said. "Ok guys, let's wrap this up."

Josh ran over to Brittany to check on her. She was dazed but okay. He said, "I'm sorry that you are having to go through this Brittany. What you did was truly brave! Thank you!"

"That's what friends do. They stand in the gap for one another," Brittany said. "Thank you, Josh!"

"For what?" he replied.

"For being a friend to me. I really need it," Brittany said.

As Cal, Brittany, and Josh came out of the house, Deborah was there to embrace both Cal and Josh. Caden ran to Brittany and embraced her. Caden then spoke to everyone, "From this day forward, HUMAN ALLIES no longer exists. I have seen what the desire for more technology can do and I am through with it."

Everyone started to cheer his announcement. Ezzie, then went over to Caden and Brittany and said, "Please come stay with us until things are worked out with your mother." Caden and Brittany looked at each other and then nodded at Ezzie.

The moment was bittersweet for Josh as he was excited that it was all over, but the pain of losing Ruth began to rush back into his mind. He walked over to where her body was as Thomas was beside her. He took off his cross and put it in her hands. "Here, the rose now blooms with you."

Thomas looked up at Josh and then said, "Josh, she was a brave woman. She went through a lot to get us here. But she is also a complete woman."

Perplexed by what Thomas said, Josh asked, "What do you mean by complete?"

Thomas explained, "You see for the believer in Jesus, death is not as much of an event as it a passing from here to eternity. The moment she breathed her last here, she was embraced by Jesus in heaven. So, while it hurts for us here, we can know that she is complete right now."

Thomas stood up and began to softly sing:
Because He lives, I can face tomorrow.
Because He lives, all fear is gone.
Because I know, He holds the future.
And life is worth the living, just because He lives.

Chapter 20

Unfinished

The atmosphere at the Den was joyous as everyone gathered. Hugs and laughter were being shared, especially to Deborah, Josh, and Cal. The stories of the events of the night were being told and celebrated as well. Josh, Yashi, and Bub, all embraced Terra as reunited friends. Cal and Deborah didn't leave each other's side as they were reunited in their marriage. Duo restored to his original identity and was able to have music playing for everyone as they watched Barry lead the group in dance moves. The group also celebrated their new arrivals of Caden, Brittany, Ryan, and Bale.

As the celebration continued, Bale stood off in the corner away from everyone. Ty walked over to him and said, "Are you going to join in?"

"Honestly, I don't know what to celebrate," Bale said. "My whole life is ruined. ProTech is forever finished. And I don't know where to go from here. I hated you all just three hours ago, and now I am here supposedly celebrating with you all. It just doesn't make sense in my mind."

"There was once someone that had the same thoughts," Ty replied.

"Really?" Bale said.

"Yeah there was once this guy similar to you," Ty said, "He thought he had the world figured out. He thought he knew better than everyone around him. So, he went out into the world and made, at first, a huge success of himself. Everyone loved being around him and his money. But with his desire to be the life of the party, it cost him. In fact, it cost him everything."

"What did he do?" Bale asked.

"He reached a point where he had nothing," Ty said. "And he thought it would be better for me to go back home than to keep living with nothing."

"I bet his family was upset that he had spent all his money," Bale said.

"In fact, it was just the opposite," Ty motioned his hand towards everyone, "His family celebrated with him. Were there some upset with him? Yeah, but the celebration of the future was greater than what he did in the past."

Ty looked at Bale and could see the tears rolling down his face. "I'm ready for a new future." Bale said slowly.

"We are too!" Ty replied with a smile.

--

After a while, Josh found himself sitting alone, reflecting on everything that had happened over the past few days. Bub, Yashi, Terra, and Brittany all came over to talk with Josh.

"Hey man, we are sorry about your grandmother," Yashi said.

"Thanks guys. It will be hard to forget her. I am grateful for each one of you," Josh said.

Bub looked at Josh and could see that there was something else on his mind, "Josh, what are you thinking about? You should be celebrating, but you look confused."

"Well," Josh replied, "It was something that my grandmother said right before she passed."

"What was it?" Terra asked.

"She said how the code was not finished yet," Josh said.

Josh wrestled some papers around and found the code that was originally written. "Do you remember the other night when she was explaining the code, she got all the way to the last line but she never fully explained it. And then for her to say that the code is not finished yet, has me wondering. Look at it again."

"40 days are over. 40 nights are not. The Rose has bloomed, remember where one was not, one is now. Two know where one is but not one."

Josh said, "Look at what it says, 'Two know where one is but not one.' She never explained that line before she was interrupted. It has to be that is what she means by finish the code.

"I wonder if she is talking about your dad, in that he didn't know where your mother was," Brittany said.

"Or maybe she is talking about you," Bub said.

"I don't think so, "Josh said, "I feel like there is something that we are missing."

Suddenly all the power in the Den went out. There was an immediate hush over the crowd as this had never happened before.

Thomas turned on a flashlight and spoke up, "It must be that the blackouts are impacting our power. I'll check on the generators."

Bale spoke up, "The blackouts were only intended to happen in Valley Hills, not outside of there. It is a separate power grid that I couldn't control. Yet."

The darkness was broken by a small screen on a computer that began to flash the words in white, "It is not finished...I am waiting."

Bale looked at Deborah and whispered, "It's Dad. Run..."

Part 3: Shutdown

The bike raced down the street, urgency in every pedal, the rider oblivious to the world around him. Swerving around a corner, a card-like flicker sounded through the wheels, and he narrowly avoided a car whose driver scolded him to slow down. Unfazed, he sped up, reaching his house on the next street. Standing on the pedals, he maneuvered until, with a swift move, he left the still-spinning bicycle on the ground and hurried to the front door.

Turning the front door knob in a rush, he almost stumbled inside, bolting up the stairs. A mother's voice warned him to slow down, but he paid no heed. Bursting into his bedroom, he found a girl at a computer.

"Did you get it?" she asked eagerly.

"Yes, somehow, I got it," he replied.

"Give it to me."

He handed her a jump drive from his pocket, and she exclaimed, "Now we can see how it works," clicking the mouse. Their attention turned to a metal hand on a table, and silence filled the room.

Suddenly, a deep roar echoed from downstairs. "Where are you?" the voice demanded.

The boy panicked, realizing he might be in trouble. The girl reassured him, "Here, get in my closet. I got this." He squeezed into the small space, watching through the slots as the girl worked on the computer.

A loud noise interrupted their focus. "Where is he?" the man shouted as he entered the room.
"Who?" the girl innocently responded.
"Where is your brother? I know he's here."
"Oh, Dad," she downplayed, "I'm sure he's somewhere here, but not where you want him to be." The clever play on words bought them a moment.
"If you see him," the man said, approaching the closet, "tell him I know what he has, and it won't work." Just as the girl distracted him, the fingers on the metal hand moved.
Ignoring her brother's safety, she guided her father away, insisting, "I'm sure whatever you have to say, he needs to hear it from you." As he was about to leave, he noticed the hand on the table.
"What is that?" he inquired.
"Just a science project," she said, attempting to divert his attention. Desperate to keep him from discovering the hidden agenda, she steered him toward the door.
But he was fixated on the hand. "Wait, I've seen that before." Picking it up, he examined it closely.
"It's a study on the structure of the hand," she explained, hoping to redirect his focus. "I think Mom has dinner almost ready."
"Unbelievable," he muttered, still captivated.
"Dad, it's time to go. I'll see you at dinner," she urged.
As he left, he mentioned, "Tell D I know it was him." She listened at the door, signaling her brother to wait.
"All clear," she declared.

He burst out, relieved. "Finally! I thought he had me that time. Thank you, sis! What am I going to do?"

"I got what I needed from the jump drive. Take it back as soon as possible."

"Okay, what was Dad talking about when he saw the hand?"

"I'm not sure." Suddenly, the hand began to move on its own.

The siblings exchanged a triumphant smile.

Chapter 21

Search History

The room was plunged into sudden chaos as piercing lights illuminated the darkness, accompanied by urgent yells commanding everyone to freeze. Figures clad in soldier attire descended upon the Den, armed with shock guns. The scene unfolded into utter pandemonium.

Ezzie hit a button that immediately broke off a piece of the stairs that descended to the bottom of the Den and began releasing smoke into the room. While this stopped the progress of the guards, they began to fire their shock guns at anyone they could target. Yet the smoke prevented them from making any accurate shots.

Ever vigilant as leaders, Ty and Thomas began hitting switches on the walls that fried the computers being used, so sparks began to go off like fireworks all around the room. Cal and Deborah began directing everyone to escape through different hidden tunnels that had been covered up by various pieces of furniture.

Abby, Cal's sister, directed Josh's friends Bub, Terra, Yashi, Ryan, and Caden to a specific tunnel. However, Brittany stopped for a moment to check on Josh. Cal and Deborah grabbed Josh and Bale and hunkered down behind a table. Josh could see Brittany looking at him with the intent to stay, but then he yelled, "Go, I will catch up with you all later." Just then, Abby's head poked out of the tunnel,

"Brittany, we have to go; he will be ok." Brittany nodded her head and disappeared into one of the tunnels.

As the sounds of shock guns continued to echo in the room with each shot, Cal ran to Josh and Bale and said with a stern tone, "Son, you have to go with Mom! Bale, you are going with me! We have to split up! They are after both of you! Move and keep your head down!"

"We will meet at the place!" Deborah said to Cal. Then she turned to Josh and said, "Josh, we are going to the bookcase in the next room."

"Are you ready?" Cal said hurriedly. "Go!"

In a military-style crawl, Josh followed his mother, Deborah, to a bookcase that had not been moved. She stood briefly, pulled on a book, and heard a latch release. Then she grabbed the bookcase and swung it open like a door; a tunnel was behind it.

As Josh looked back, he overheard one of the soldiers say, "Come on, let's get them." He could see how they began to exit from the top of the Den since there was no hope of their coming to the bottom.

When they were in the tunnel, Deborah pulled the bookcase close behind her. The tunnel was at first dark, and she reached over and hit a button that turned on a small strip of lights that dimly lit a pathway for them to follow. Josh noticed her pause and could see one more switch beside the light switch. He could hear her say, "All this time and all this work! Lord, you are my Shield and Defender!" When she flipped the switch, she looked at Josh and said, "Come on, let's go!"

The switch set off another chain reaction of minor explosives hidden in the Den's walls, which began to cause the walls to collapse upon one another. Filling in the space entirely and causing the lighthouse to start to crumble on top.

As Josh and Deborah hurried through the tunnel, not knowing where it would end, he could tell she had prepared for this moment. When they reached a particular place, Josh noticed another set of switches. She stopped and looked at her watch. She counted and whispered, "5...4...3...2...1." Then she flipped the switch, and you could hear more rumbling, this time within the tunnel. She said, "Just a little more, let's go!" Then she took off again.

They continued to wind through all the tunnels when Josh could notice ahead how the lights were ending, and the tunnel looked to come to a stop. But there was a ladder. When they ran to the ladder, he noticed a small canvas bag hanging by it. Deborah motioned back to Josh for him to stop, then moved her fingers to her lips to stay quiet. She grabbed the bag, threw it over her shoulder, and began climbing up the ladder quietly, pausing at the top to listen for any soldiers present. Slowly, she lifted a hatch and looked around cautiously. She looked down at Josh, motioned with her hand for him to come, and whispered, "Ok, the coast is clear."

When Josh poked his head out of the top, he was in a part of the woods he had never been in. It was a part that Cal and Deborah warned him not to go through with the friends as there may be someone watching them in them. He realized, however, that this was their way to escape, and the friends could have messed up their plans if they ever found the hatches.

Deborah immediately reached inside the bag, pulled out a walkie-talkie, and put it inside its batteries. Josh noticed other random items in the bag, but she quickly closed it back. She looked at Josh and urgently said, "Son, we are not finished yet. We must go a little further to ensure we are all safe. Are you ok?" Josh, without hesitation, said, "Yes, ma'am."

"Ok, let's begin to move." Deborah said as she looked down at her watch again, "But if you see me tell you to stop or be quiet, you have to do exactly what I say, no questions asked. Do you understand?" Josh had never seen this side of his mother and again said, "Yes, ma'am."

Deborah and Josh then began to go through the woods along some paths on the ground. They looked worn down like someone had been going on them before or even preparing for them. He looked off in the distance and could see another lighthouse, with its light shining toward them, providing an ambiance of enough light to help them see where they were going.

At a certain point, Deborah stopped and motioned for Josh to halt his progress. She looked around to ensure no one was coming as Josh realized they had come to a road. Suddenly, Deborah pulled Josh to the ground behind a large rock and said sternly, "Get down and be quiet!"

A large truck was coming with bright lights. It began to go past them, and the words ProTech were written on the side. Suddenly, you heard a voice yell in a military tone, "STOP!" The truck screeched its tires and came to an immediate stop. Josh's heart began to race as he was sure they would get caught.

"He should be up this way," the soldier yelled as he motioned in the direction from where they had just come. "Keep your eyes up and your shock guns on." Slowly, the soldiers began working through the woods while the truck remained on the road.

Slowly, Josh saw Deborah reach into her bag, and there was a box that had a button on it with an antenna. She then turned, clicked the button on the walkie-talkie, and had her ear up to the radio to listen. Rather than hearing someone speak, she would hear the sound of someone else clicking their button, which made a muffled sound for her. She began to count after each one happened, "1...2...3..." Then she paused, and her countenance changed. "Where's four?" She said to herself with concern in her tone. She then grabbed the radio, clicked the button four times a row, and waited. Silence. She began to look back.

The faint sound of yelling began to echo louder through the woods. Deborah and Josh could hear a play-by-play of what the soldiers were doing on the radios of the truck. "Bringing them out!" came through on the radio.

Bringing who out? Josh thought to himself. Suddenly, the sounds became louder and louder as the soldiers returned to the truck. There were two people with black covers over their heads and handcuffs on. At first, Josh and Deborah couldn't make out because of the shadows. However, as they came to the back of the truck, Josh looked at their shoes and realized that Cal, Ryan, and Bale had been captured.

Josh stood up to move towards the truck to try to do something, but Deborah grabbed his arm and forcefully pulled him back into hiding. Josh whispered, "We have to help him." Deborah replied, "Hold on." The lead soldier was standing in the back of the truck where they were getting ordered into the back of the car. Another soldier approached him and said, "Sir, we couldn't find the boy or any others. What do you want us to do?"

"This will be good enough for now." The lead soldier replied, "We at least got the one he wanted for him. The other is just a bonus. Let's go, and we will return and look for the others later. He will tell us where they are."

Then, with military precision, the truck drove off with Cal, Ryan, and Bale in the back.

Josh began to cry as he realized there was nothing he tried to do to stop them. He looked at Deborah and saw how emotional she was, shocked at what happened. "The plan was perfect." She said to herself. "I don't know what we missed and how they knew we were here." She then grabbed the box with the switch and clicked the button. A low rumble echoed through the woods. "What just happened?" Josh asked. "It was the final step of the escape plan," Deborah said, with her countenance now being one of grief and confusion. "The Den is finished."

She looked at Josh, grasped his arm, and said, "We have to cross here and go a little further." Josh ripped his arm away from her grasp and replied, "But what about Dad? What about Bale? We need to go after them."

"We alone can't do anything to save them; we need everyone's help."

"Everyone, there is no more everyone. The Den is gone!" Josh sat down on a rock and put his head in his hands.

"Shh!" Deborah said, reminding him to stay quiet. "Trust me! We will find and save them, but we must keep going for now."

Josh reluctantly stood up with her and kept moving forward into the woods.

They came to a specific clearing with large rocks resting on one another along the edge.

Deborah grabbed her walkie-talkie and said softly, "5 is here." Then, surprised, a large rock slowly rolled to the side. A small light began to break through the darkness of the clearing. "All clear!" came from inside, which sounded like Aunt Abby. Deborah then slipped between the rocks into the darkness between the stones. She whispered back, "Josh, come, it is safe."

Josh ducked behind the rock and looked back to see Abby rolling the rock back into place. When he turned around, he was handed a flashlight by Deborah. "Come this way." She said, "Stay along the wall."

As they moved forward and Josh moved his flashlight around, he could begin to make out the massive cavern that they were in. They walked through some water, and he could then make out dim lights that were getting brighter as they lit up the entire space.

The room looked similar to the Den. Some computers were there. There were even rooms surrounding the ample open space that looked like places for people to sleep in. The room had small tables and benches around it. Then, there was a radio system that was turned on. When he walked into the lit room of the cave, all his friends were huddled beside a fire that was being used to keep everyone warm. Yashi looked up and noticed that Josh was present. "Josh!" He yelled out, and then all the friends turned their attention to him being in the room and rushed over to embrace him. He was relieved to see his friends. Deborah was embraced by Ty, Thomas, and Ezzie.

Terra said, "Josh, where are your dad and Bale?" Before Josh could reply, Deborah interjected and announced, "I am glad we are all safe here. Cal and Bale have been caught by ProTech." The room was filled with gasps and "Oh no." The friends looked at Josh with shock at what they heard with his gaze towards the floor.

"For now, we are safe here!" Deborah continued, "That is what we need to know. Ty, Thomas, Ezzie, and Abby, let's meet." As she nodded towards another room in the cave, they began to walk that way.

Josh turned to his friends, and Bub said, "Dude, I can't believe they have your dad. It must have been Bale who gave us all up. He was letting them know where the Den was the entire time."

"I don't think this was Bale," Josh replied. "We overheard the guards discussing how a man will be happy they caught them."

"It must be Aiden." Brittany chimed in.

"Aiden, who's that?" Yashi asked.

"Aiden is our oldest brother," Caden said. "He works for ProTech and Bale."

"Why are we just hearing about him?" Bub asked.

"Well, Aiden was just a developer who worked in the offices. He has never been someone of influence." Caden replied.

"Until?" Brittany interjected.

"Until when?" Josh asked.

"Aiden was working on a new software that could track people without them knowing it," Brittany said. "His software would have made him a major influencer at ProTech, and he must have just finished it."

"Oh great, now we have to deal with Belliston's 2.0," Terra said sarcastically.

Brittany turned to Josh, "I'm sorry, Josh, I had no idea how much Aiden would be involved. I can talk to him if you want him to stop."

"No, it's not your fault, Brittany," Josh replied as he sat down. "What done is done! We have to figure out a way to save my dad and Bale. I need to talk with my mom."

Josh slipped away from the friends and moved outside the room where the adults were meeting. He could overhear their conversation.

"I just can't figure out how they knew our location," Ty said in frustration.

"I know." Josh interrupted. "It's Aiden Belliston. Without his knowledge, he created a tracking software that must be planted on Bale. At least, that's what Brittany says."

"A tracking software? Oh no, that means everything we could be down here forever." Abby cried.

"I need to talk with my mom," Josh replied.

Deborah nodded in agreement, and the others left the room.

"Mom, I don't think this is Aiden Belliston," Josh said.

"But you just said..." Deborah replied

"I know, but I needed someone to blame momentarily."

"Who then do you think is responsible for this?"

"I think it was Bale, but I can't prove it."

"Honey, I believe my brother is a changed man."

"I know, but what if it was just a way for him to get closer to all of us."

"I know that you have had your fights with Bale," Deborah said as she put her hand on Josh's shoulder. "But Bale is not the enemy on this one."

"Then who is?" Josh asked.

Suddenly, Thomas entered the room, "Deborah and Josh, you need to hear this…"

Everyone was standing around the radio and could hear the vague sound of talking coming through it. As Thomas adjusted the dial to bring it into tune, it became more straightforward to understand.

"Protectors…Protectors…" It was a different voice. "It's time to come out from hiding. I can find you if you don't. Tell D I know it was her. You have 24 hours."

"What does that mean?" Ty asked. "Tell D I know it was her?"

"Let's all calm down," Thomas interjected.

"Mom, what's wrong?" Josh looked at her face and could see her in complete shock.

"I know who it is," Deborah said.

"Is it Bale?" Josh asked.

"No, it's worse!" Deborah began to crack her voice in worry. "It's your grandfather."

Chapter 22

Key Code

The ride was longer than expected. The conversation among the soldiers in the back of the truck was based on plans for the weekend in Valley Hills. Soon, however, the truck stopped, and the tone of the conversation changed to being orders.

"Stand up! Get out of the truck!" became the repeated phrase repeatedly to Bale, Ryan, and Cal. Still with their head coverings on, they were roughly escorted out of the truck. Not knowing where they were, Bale realized that the group was split between Cal, Ryan, and himself. He could tell that he ended up being walked down a hall. Suddenly, he was thrown into a seat, and the covering was removed from his head. A bright light glared into his eyes, and he noticed a figure standing behind the light.

"You just had to leave, didn't you." The deep voice echoed in the room.

Bale, still being handcuffed, couldn't use his hands to cover the blinding light, so he was left trying to guess the source of the voice.

"You had it all," the voice bellowed with a tone of disappointment, "And you were willing to walk away."

"Broderick, is that you?" Bale tried to get an idea of who was behind the voice.

"Broderick, ha," the voice burst with a sarcastic chuckle. "He was weak and didn't know how to protect himself."

"And you have become weak as well, Dek," the voice growled.

"Dad?" Bale's voice cracked with fear.

"Yes, son. It's your dear ole daddy, Victor. I haven't gone anywhere yet." Victor said with a crafty smile.

"Where have you been?" Bale asked.

"Here!" Victor replied. "In my home watching everything. Funding everything. Making sure that we had this moment right here."

"How?"

"Look around, son." Victor turned off the light and motioned his arms for Bale to look around the room.

As Bale's eyes adjusted, he began to see the most modern room he had ever seen. In the corner was a workbench with numerous hardware boards on it. There was his large desk. There was even a hologram phone system that was used.

"I have created the most protected organization ever," Victor replied. "All those years that you were playing around making your technology, I was the one making sure that the deals went through. I was the one making sure that you kept moving forward. I provided you with the board and contracts. It was me, not you! And I could watch every step you took, even to this day. That is why finding you in that Den tunnel with Cal was so easy."

"And what about Mom in all of this?" Bale asked.

"Unfortunately, we didn't see eye-to-eye on what was important. She was a very gracious woman, but her graciousness wasn't compatible with my efficiency. I truly hated to hear of her passing even though we disagreed." Victor paused for a moment as if he was reflecting on her. Suddenly, there was a knock on the door. A man came walking into the room and brought a tray of glasses of water and a pitcher. He set them down on the coffee table. Bale vaguely looked at the man and thought for a second that he recognized him.

"Bale, meet Japheth!" as he motioned towards him, "He's Noah 2.0," Victor said.

"He's a robot?" Bale asked.

Bale looked at Japheth and saw the humanlike characteristics he had never seen before. He stared again as he was sure that he recognized the robot.

"How did you do this?" Bale looked intently at Japheth.

"It was my new program called Generations," Victor replied. "Oh, Japheth, take off Bale's handcuffs. We won't need those anymore." Japheth walked over behind Bale, and he could snap the steel and remove it in one grasp of the handcuffs.

"Japheth is my newest prototype. He is going to change the world. Shoot, he is going to soon be what the world is."

"Be what the world is?" Bale asked.

"Look closely at him. Who do you see?" Victor asked.

Bale broadened his eyes and realized he was looking into Broderick's face.

"How did this happen? Broderick is in jail." Bale asked.

"I told you it's my new program called Generations," Victor said with almost a sheepish grin.

"You see, Dek, why should someone's abilities like Broderick's be hindered for wanting to help me?" Victor asked.

"So, I can take someone's DNA from prison and turn them into this," motioning towards Japheth. "But this is better than what it was. No conscience in this one, just obedience."

"So, is your plan to create one for everyone?" Bale asked.

"If I have to," Victor said confidently.

"But what about the people?" Bale asked.

"Did you hear what I said, Dek?" Victor asked. "If this continues to work, why will there be a need for people!" You could just live on through this for generations to come. Generations with no need for problems, sickness, or finances. Just complete obedience to what I think and say."

"You've gone mad," Bale exclaimed.

"No, son, I have gone efficient; efficiency means power. I am unsure if that is something you ever understood, son." Victor said.

"Your sister didn't understand it. Neither does that weird husband, Cal. But that will all change soon."

"How?"

"Leverage, my boy. Leverage!"

"What do you mean by leverage?"

"Dek, it is time to decide what part of history you want to be on. Do you want to be on the side of power, or do you want to be on the side of those pathetic Protectors?"

"But Deborah, Cal, and Josh, your own family are on that side! Mom was on that side!"

"Son, I want them to see how they can join us. We can all be in control together for generations to come."
"What are you asking me to do?"
"I want you to find Josh for me. That's it."
"Josh, why not Deborah?"
"Josh is the key to the Generations program's success."
Bale asked, "And why should I help you? You've been gone this entire time. What difference will it make?"
"You see all of this," motioning around the room and to his outside compound, "it will be yours, my son."
Suddenly, Japheth entered back into the room. "Sir, you have a call." Victor walked over to the holographic unit and Aiden Belliston's image came up.
"Sir, we are ready to begin" Aiden said with a confident smirk on his face. "Soon the Protectors will be no more."
"Excellent, Aiden. I always appreciate how you follow through." Victor turned his face towards Bale as he spoke. Bale dropped his head in shame.
"Let it begin!" Victor said.
"Son, do you see how easy this can be for you?" Victor said as he moved back to his desk in front of Bale.
"And what if I say no?" Bale replied.
"No! That sounds like a word that Cal would say. Bring up room 3 screen." Suddenly, it showed on the screen Cal sitting in the room in a chair with a covering over his head. Two guards came into the room, pulled out rods, and began to shock Cal over and over.

Victor said aloud, "Room 3." the guards stopped momentarily and looked at the camera.

Bale noticed Broderick's face in the guards.

"Again!" Victor growled.

The guards began to shock Cal again, causing him to fall to the floor as he was crying out in pain.

"Do you see the impact of obedience versus conscience, my boy?" Victor chimed.

The sight was too much for Bale, so he cried, "Stop! Please stop! I will help you find Josh."

Chapter 23

Generations

The Protectors gathered deep within the concealed cavern, their faces etched with concern and determination. The flickering candles cast shadows on their focused expressions as they discussed the imminent threat posed by Victor and the urgent need for a strategic response. Bub, the group's joker, lightened the tension as he declared, "I need a bag of chips. My sugar is low."
Terra, the ever-practical voice of reason, responded, "I don't think chips will help your sugar levels. Aren't you concerned about what is happening?"
Bub, undeterred, quipped, "Yes, I'm concerned, but we are kids being chased by an army. I trust the Protectors. We took down Bale, and we can take down any army."
Yashi, exuding a refreshing confidence, chimed in, "Absolutely. We have the skills and unity to face whatever comes our way."
Caden then said, "This is different. Almost more powerful than I have seen."
Brittany drifted over to where Josh was sitting at the end of the table. "Are you ok?"
Josh seemed unresponsive and was staring at the candles flickering in the darkness, grappling with the weight of the situation. Suddenly, a hand rested on his shoulder. He turned to see his mother, Deborah,

who knelt down with a look filled with concern and determination. "Your grandfather, Victor, is behind all of this. He's the one we need to stop."

Josh's eyes widened. "Grandfather? Victor? But why?"

"He's after something, Josh. He sees power in controlling people through technology and will go to extreme lengths to achieve it. We need to find a way to stop him," Deborah explained.

Terra, crossing her arms, added, "If anyone can figure out a way to stop him, it's us. We've faced challenges before, and we'll face them again."

Ty interjected with urgency, "We heard a message from Cal. Victor has him captive, and he's using him as leverage to get us to cooperate. He wants us to find you, Josh."

Josh's mind raced. "What do we do? How can we save Dad and Bale?"

Deborah took a deep breath. "We need a plan. We can't let Victor control us or use us against each other. We need to get everyone but carefully and strategically."

Abby said, "First, we need to understand Victor's motives better. Ezzie, can you hack into ProTech's systems and gather intel on Victor's plans?"

Ezzie, focused on her laptop, nodded. "I'll do my best. If we can find out more about his operations, we might be able to exploit weaknesses."

Bub raised an eyebrow, injecting humor into the tense atmosphere, "Exploit weaknesses? That's my kind of plan!"

Deborah shot him a look. "We need to be serious, Bub. Lives are at stake here."

"Right, right," Bub muttered, feigning seriousness.
Deborah continued, "In the meantime, Ty and Thomas need to assess our resources. We've lost the Den, but we still have each other. We can't let fear paralyze us."
Barry, always eager for adventure, enthusiastically said, "I like the sound of this. Count me in."
Thomas added, "We should establish communication channels that Victor can't easily trace. We can't risk him finding us again."
Feeling determined, Josh declared, "I want to help. I can't let them win."
Deborah rose, putting her hands on Josh's shoulders, conveying motherly love and determination. "We'll need all of us! We are the Protectors, remember. But, Josh, we have to keep you out of sight. Victor seems fixated on you for some reason. We have to figure out why."
"But Mom, I have to do something," Josh retorted.
"Josh, they are after you. You should stay here," Deborah said commandingly.
Deborah then joined Ty, Thomas, Ezzie, and Abby as they huddled up, strategizing on their next moves.
"There's something I have to do," Josh said to himself, unable to ignore the call to action.
Ezzie, amid her digital investigation, suddenly shouted, "I think I have something. I went back to Bale's network." She showcased her skills, accessing encrypted files, navigating through firewalls, and delving into the digital labyrinth he had created.
Ty pointed at a file labeled "Generations." "What's that?"

When Ezzie attempted to access it, a password prompt appeared. "It has the Destroyer code," she explained. "If you get it wrong, it erases the file completely. The only way to bypass the code is to access it is on its server."

Abby pondered, "What could be the password, a backdoor into systems, or something else?"

Looking at the file on the screen, Deborah began to say under her breath, "Generations… I have heard that before."

Deborah's eyes narrowed. "Generations…must be the core of his plan. We need to discover the nature of this project and find a way to dismantle it."

Ty said, "While Ezzie continues digging, let's focus on how to get Cal and Bale back. We can't afford any mishaps."

Thomas added, "And we need to establish a secure communication network. We can't let Victor intercept our messages."

The Protectors began to divide their tasks, each member contributing to the collective effort to thwart Victor's plans.

Deborah looked back from the huddle and said, "Josh, do you want to help?"

But when they looked back, Josh wasn't sitting at the table. His friends were just as shocked that Josh wasn't there anymore.

"Josh…Josh…" Deborah began to look around the cave. "Everyone stop and look. We have to find Josh!"

In the quiet cavern, the Protectors joined the search for Josh. His absence raised concern, and they knew they needed to find him before it was too late.

Meanwhile, Josh had slipped out of the cave, understanding the gravity of the situation and feeling compelled to warn others.

Chapter 24

Viral

Josh's phone buzzed with a notification, "A new video from Spot-On President Aiden Belliston was just released…"
Intrigued, Josh clicked on the link.
Aiden Belliston stood resolutely in front of a black background.
My fellow Spot-On friends of Valley Hills and the world. We live in unprecedented times, and our way of life is constantly threatened. While I wish the threat was from those outside Valley Hills, unfortunately, they exist from within. Some want us to go back. Some fear progress. Some are afraid of change. My friends, ProTech is here to ensure that Valley Hills continues to be the place of innovation for all the world.
For those who are scared of progress, the Protectors, this is my official warning. There is no place you can hide. There is no reason for you to try to hinder the advancement of ProTech and its resources.
For those who know the Protectors, please be sure that you know that to help them means that you are guilty as well. You will be removed as well.
So, friends, I am announcing the search for any Protectors each night. Anyone found to be a Protector will be removed. Anyone found to be helping them will be removed. But until the Protectors are removed, the alarms will continue.
The next day, the hallways of Valley Hills High School buzzed with the energy of students transitioning between classes. Amid the typical

chaos of lockers slamming and laughter echoing, Josh navigated the school urgently. Aiden Belliston's video had spread like wildfire, and the atmosphere in the school had shifted.

As Josh moved through the halls, he noticed a heightened level of surveillance. Security personnel patrolled the corridors, taking Aiden's video seriously.

Suddenly, a door cracked open, and a whisper beckoned for Josh's attention. "Come in here," he heard from the darkened room.

Realizing the need to avoid the hallways, Josh entered the room. His collar was grasped and pulled in with a mighty tug, the door closing immediately.

"Nunley, what are you doing here?" The words slightly lisped as Josh tried to adjust to the darkness. Then, a small light revealed radios and computers in the room. It was Sylvester.

"Sylvester? What are you doing in here?" Josh asked.

"I was working on a project, and then I heard the announcement on Spot-On. I thought that if I was Josh, I would want to come warn friends at school."

"So, you aren't going to turn me in?"

"No! I believe, too, Josh! Do you remember when we talked in the library? I began to explore Noah in the Bible, and I realized that God was powerful enough to help Noah; he must be powerful enough to save even the worst of us!"

Josh was amazed at Sylvester's revelation.

"Josh, you are in danger and must get out of here."

"I know, but I have to warn Ellie and Tad," Josh said. "We've got to do something. Aiden's video is spreading like crazy, and people are turning against the Protectors," Josh urgently whispered.

Sylvester frowned; his concern mirrored in his eyes. "What can we do? Aiden has the Belliston influence behind him. It's like a tidal wave of public opinion."

"I need to warn Ellie," Josh said. "Can you find her and tell her to meet me in the library?"

Sylvester nodded. "Alright, I'll find Ellie and make sure she's safe. But we've got to be careful. Aiden's got the teachers in his pocket."

He slowly cracked open the door and motioned for Josh to wait. Sylvester then began to move and signaled for Josh to follow him.

"She's in math currently, I believe," Josh whispered.

"Ok." Sylvester.

Josh stopped Sylvester briefly and said, "Thanks."

Sylvester slipped down the hallway.

Finally, Sylvester located Ellie in math class. She was engrossed in her studies. He tried to motion for her attention, but she continued to look down at her work.

"Mr. Sylvester! Are you going to join the math class?"

Sylvester let out a screech of surprise. He turned around, and it was Mr. Rodriguez, the new principal.

"Oh, sorry, Mr. Rodriguez." Sylvester tried to reply while covering up his nervousness.

"What do you need, Mr. Sylvester?"

"I need to give a message to Ellie."

"A message from whom?"

"Uhm…" Sylvester looked for the words to say. "Her brother."
"And what is the message?"
"Her brother, Josh, wants her to go to the library today."
"That's it?"
"Yes, that's it!"
"I will give her the message then."
"No!" Sylvester responded nervously. "I can do it."
Shocked at Sylvester's response, Mr. Rodriguez replied, "No, Mr. Sylvester, I will give it to her. It's time for you to get back to class."
"Yes, sir!" Sylvester slumped his shoulders and then slowly moved away.
Mr. Rodriguez poked his head into the classroom and had the teacher send Ellie into the hallway.
"Mr. Sylvester wanted me to give you a message."
"Sylvester?" Ellie asked.
"He said it is from your brother, Josh."
Puzzled, Ellie thought for a moment. Then she realized it was from Josh but decided not to give it to Mr. Rodriguez.
"Oh yeah, my brother Josh!" She replied. "What's the message?"
Just as confused, Mr. Rodriguez said, "Your brother wants you to go to the library for him today."
"Oh great!" Ellie replied. "Will do! Thank you, Mr. Rodriguez!"
After class, Ellie slipped into the library. She went to a desk in the corner. Josh approached her cautiously, not wanting to cause a scene. Sylvester kept watch for any signs of trouble.
"Ellie, we need to talk," Josh said quietly, glancing around to ensure no one was eavesdropping.

Ellie looked up, concern etched on her face. "What's going on?"

"Aiden Belliston made a video blaming the Protectors for everything. It's spreading like crazy, and people are starting to believe it. We need to be careful," Josh explained.

Ellie's eyes widened in disbelief. "But that's not true! We've been trying to help people, not cause trouble."

"I know, Ellie. We have to stay vigilant and watch out for each other. Aiden's influence is strong, and we can't underestimate what he might do," Josh cautioned.

As they continued their conversation, the librarian approached, eyeing them suspiciously. "Keep it down, you two. This is a place of study."

They nodded and dispersed, trying to blend into the library's quiet atmosphere.

"I have to save my father and Bale," Josh whispered. "Can you help me?"

"Yes, what do you need?" Ellie Grace asked.

"Does your dad still work in the building maintenance for ProTech?"

"Yes!"

"There is someone behind ProTech, and it's not Bale or Belliston."

"You mean someone even more powerful?"

"Yes, it's my grandfather, Victor. I need to find him. They have Bale and my father, and they are threatening all of us."

"Let me see what I can find out."

"Be careful. My grandfather is very powerful."

Their conversation was interrupted, with Sylvester whispering, "The bell is about to ring for the next period."

Josh stood up and put his hood back over his head, "Thank you for your help, and be careful who you trust."

Ellie Grace said with a tone of concern, "Be careful."

The bell suddenly rang as they gazed at each other for a moment. Josh picked up his backpack and began to slip away.

Unbeknownst to Josh and Ellie, Mr. Rodriguez had been monitoring the situation closely.

Mr. Rodriguez discreetly followed Josh after he left the library, watching from a distance. When Josh approached the next hallway, Mr. Rodriguez seized the opportunity.

"Josh Nunley, a word, please," Mr. Rodriguez said sternly.

Josh turned, surprised by the principal's sudden appearance and the fact that he recognized him. "Come with me."

In Mr. Rodriguez's office, the stern-faced principal sat behind his desk, eyeing Josh with suspicion and concern.

"What's going on, Josh? I've been hearing troubling things about the Protectors. Aiden Belliston's video has stirred quite a storm," Mr. Rodriguez said.

Josh took a deep breath, choosing his words carefully. "Sir, Aiden's video is misleading. The Protectors are not to blame for everything. We've been trying to make a positive difference in Valley Hills."

Mr. Rodriguez leaned back in his chair, crossing his arms. "This situation is getting out of hand. Aiden is convincing people that the Protectors are a threat. What am I supposed to do?"

Josh pleaded, "You have to understand, sir. Aiden is manipulating the truth. The Protectors are here to help, not harm."

The principal sighed, running a hand through his hair. "Josh, you're putting me in a difficult position. I've got pressure from influential people to cooperate. I need to decide and can't afford to make enemies."

Realizing the gravity of the situation, Josh thought quickly. "If you're concerned about making enemies, sir, know that Aiden is not the person you should be aligning with. He's using his influence to manipulate and control. You need to look beyond the surface and see the truth."

Mr. Rodriguez seemed torn, caught between his duty and the conflicting interests pulling at him. Finally, he sighed, "I need time to think. But for now, Josh, you need to go with me. I've been instructed to take you to the Bellistons."

Josh's heart sank. He had hoped to sway the principal, but it seemed Aiden's influence reached even the highest levels of authority in the school. As Mr. Rodriguez escorted Josh out of the office, Sylvester, who had been discreetly watching, ran back to his darkened room and got on the radio to try and contact the Protectors.

"Stay close, Sylvester. We'll find a way to get Josh back. We can't let him fall into the hands of the Bellistons," Thomas instructed.

"Wait a second, I have an idea," Sylvester confidently replied.

Meanwhile, Mr. Rodriguez escorted Josh through the school corridors to the primary office doors. As they neared the exit, suddenly, the fire alarm went off.

The radio on Mr. Rodriguez's hip began to sound off. "Mr. Rodriguez, we have smoke from the old janitor's closet.

At the same time, a figure emerged behind them— Tim, the janitor.

"Mr. Rodriguez, I'll take it from here," Tim said with a smile.
Mr. Rodriguez hesitated, glancing between Josh and Tim.
"Go and check on the smoke," Tim said.
"Keep him here and wait for Belliston's men to come and get him."
Mr. Rodriguez fired off the instructions as he rushed towards the fire.
"I'm on the way." Mr. Rodriguez shouted on the radio.
Tim pulled Josh out the door and said, "Hurry, Belliston men are on the way. Get in this car. He's an old friend."
For a moment, Josh forgot that Tim was a robot.
He reached in and put a destination in the car GPS. "Hurry with no stops and no tracing."
He opened the door for Josh to be in the driver's seat. "Thomas will meet you there! Your friend Sylvester is brave!"
"Thank you, Tim!"
The car drove off and sped to the cave.
As Josh rode in the car, he noticed the signs being posted all over the city with the words "PROTECTORS" and a large red X through them. Other signs read, "No more PROTECTORS." He was fearful as every screen repeated Aiden Belliston's video. He couldn't wait to get back to the cave.

Chapter 25

Incognito Mode

When the car arrived, Josh got out, and Thomas and Deborah were there to greet him. Immediately after Josh got out and closed the door, the car began to speed off on its own back toward town.

"Are you ok?" Thomas asked

"Yes!" Josh replied.

Deborah pulled him in for a hug, and then her tone changed, "What were you thinking? I told you that you have to be careful."

"I don't know, I just wanted to help."

"Were you followed?" Thomas asked.

"No, Tim helped me to get here," Josh said.

Their conversation was broken by the crescendo sounds of the alarms going off in Valley Hills. They were close enough that the sounds were piercing for the Protectors in the cave, and the realization of them being targeted was becoming a reality.

Panic slowly began to set in. Thomas slipped into the cave and shouted orders amidst the chaos, directing everyone to calm down.

"This is not a time for panic. We must stick to our plan."

Josh's arrival in the cave was met first with a hug by Brittany. "Where did you go?"

"I had to warn people back at school," Josh replied.

"Who did you talk to?"

"Sylvester and Ellie Grace."

"Sylvester?" Bub asked.

"Ellie Grace?" Brittany asked.

"Yes, they are my friends and believe like us," Josh replied with a defense in his voice.

"Sylvester?" Bub asked again in shock.

"What else did you see?" Terra asked.

"The town is against all Protectors," Josh replied. "We have to be careful."

Suddenly, a sound broke through the radio. "Two of Everything. Come in. Two of Everything."

"Who is this?" Abby asked.

Josh stopped her. "Don't turn it off. That is Ellie Grace."

Abby began to move the dial back and forth to make it clearer.

Abby pressed the talk button twice to signal Ellie Grace to give her announcement.

The announcement came through, "Two of Everything. This is the code name Egg. The cave is compromised. The new den is on Cokesbury Lane past Spinner's Cove. Repeat, the cave is compromised. The new den is on Cokesbury Lane past Spinner's Cove."

"A new den at Cokesbury Lane?" Thomas asked.

Deborah replied. "It's a trap."

Josh replied, "No, it's where Victor is located. I had Ellie Grace to help me find it."

"Where can we go?" Caden asked.

"We need to get out of here. We can't escape the entire town." Ezzie said.

"We need to spread out and go to Martinsville, the next town over. Desirae and Bradley have a second home there." Thomas said.

"What about the computers and equipment?" Abby asked.

"Take what you can and leave the rest. We have to go." Thomas said.

"We have a problem though!" Thomas said.

"The only road to Martinsville is on the other side of Valley Hills. We will have to make it through the city undetected. The best plan is to split up and arrive separately at the bridge at Inkling Lane."

"Thomas…" the sound was from outside the cave.

Everyone rushed outside the cave to find Ty standing outside, looking in the darkness.

"There!" Ty pointed to a series of small lights piercing through the darkness. "Those aren't flashlights, they are headlights."

"Everyone back inside," Thomas said. Cautiously, they watched as the headlights sped closer to the cave.

The roar of the vehicle started to be combined with the sound of music. Bub began to step out of the cave.

"Get back in here!" Ty said.

"Why? That's not the Bellistons, that's my brother!"

The vehicle slid to an immediate stop through the dirt. The door suddenly slid open to Barry exploding out the side of the van with music roaring to a pose like a rock star.

"It's time for Adventures with Barry again, little bro!" Barry shouted.

Bub went up and did a handshake with his brother that they had rehearsed before.

"Why are you here?" Thomas asked.

"I got word from Sly Sylvester. That dude is awesome! His gameplay is awesome! I can never beat him at chess. It's like playing Magnus all over again."

"Sly Sylvester?" Bub asked.

"Yeah, he's in bro! There was this one time at school that I…"

Josh interrupted Barry's story: "What have you heard?"

"I heard you guys are in a pinch and need a Barry Broscape!"

"Barry Broscape?" Caden asked.

"Yeah, where one bro helps another bro to escape." Yashi replied.

"That's right, sushi bro!" Barry said as he pointed to him and did a different handshake.

"Sushi bro, that's offensive!" Abby said.

"What? We both like to eat sushi, and Yash man can put them dragon rolls down!" Barry replied. "Bub, I am beginning to question your friend vibe here."

"They are cool," Bub replied, looking around with his hands as if to calm everyone down. "We are all cool, right?"

Thomas said, "It's time to get everyone back inside."

When they got inside the cave, everyone circled up. Thomas began to direct everyone, "We need to protect Josh. So, he needs to be with one of us adults if we will make it to the bridge."

"Honestly, bro, I think that's a whack idea." Barry sounded off. "It's been the kids that can get around the best. So far, when he is with the adults, he gets caught."

"He's right!" Deborah said. "The kids need to go with Barry, and the adults need to split up. We can all make it on our own, but there will be a better chance if all the kids are together, so as much as I don't want to say it, the kids need to go with Barry, including Josh."

"So be it!" Thomas said. "We need to go!"

Deborah moved to Josh and pulled him apart separately as the group began to split into smaller groups. "I know that I promised you that we would never leave each other's side. But we have to for our own safety. I will see you at the bridge."

Josh hugged his mother with a longer embrace.

As they separated, Brittany was standing behind Deborah. Josh moved to her. Before she began to speak, Josh moved in and gave her a kiss on the lips. He said, "I know we are going to be together with Barry, but I want you to know I am here for you."

Brittany pulled back with shock on her face from what had just happened. Almost speechless, she said, "I'm here for you too."

As he began walking outside, Caden stood with arms crossed with Terra and Yashi watching. "We will have to talk about this later," Caden replied as a responsible older brother.

"Yeah, ya'll will," Terra chimed in sarcastically.

As they got outside, Thomas got everyone together and had them circle up for prayer:

"Lord, you are with us! Thank you! Now we ask that we go with you! Please protect us and show us Your way! In Jesus name, amen!"

Ezzie, Abby, Ty, Deborah, and Caden, led by Thomas, began to drift into the darkness of the woods. Josh entered the van with Barry, Bub, Terra, Yashi, and Brittany and began to speed off down the road.

As they fled through the winding streets, Thomas communicated with the other group via encrypted channels. "Stay low, stay hidden. We'll meet at the bridge, and from there, we'll go to Martinsville."

Almost unaware of his need to continue to drive, Barry began his conversation with Josh in the backseat. "Dude, have you seen the channel lately? I started a new channel called Breaking Stuff with Barry. It's where I find stuff to break and see how long it takes me. We already have up to a million views on Spot-On. How's it going with you, Bub's bro?"

"Just trying to find Dad and Bale. My grandfather has them kidnapped." Josh replied.

"Dude, that's heavy!" Barry had a moment of solemnness in his voice followed by silence.

As they drove past a road, there began to be lights behind the van. Barry looked in the rearview mirror and began to say, "We got some company."

"How did they find us?" Yashi asked.

"I don't know, but we must lose them," Barry said. He pressed down on the gas pedal, and the van took off. Fortunately, Barry knew many of the backroads and could drive faster than usual. As they got closer to the city, traffic surrounded them. It was risky as it would draw attention, but it was the only option to try and get rid of whoever was trying to chase them down. As they came to a part of the city, Barry ran through a red light and then made an immediate right turn and turned off his lights in the alley. Everyone looked out the back of the van to see if the car chasing them would stop or go on by. Barry whispered, "Everyone get down." They all dropped their heads down and saw the car drive past their street. For a moment, everyone let out a sigh of relief.

"Uh oh," Bub said.

Everyone turned their attention to the front of the van, and a black van was sitting there as if they were prepared for Barry to be there. They turned on their lights, so they blinded everyone. Barry knew that if he tried to escape, it would be a significant risk trying to back out on the street with traffic. A man exited the van and shouted, "Everyone get out of the van."

"What do we do?" Brittany asked.

"How did they find us?" Terra chimed in.

"Let's do what they say," Josh said as he slid open the door and got out with his hands up in surrender while trying to cover his face from the brightness of the light.

"Josh! You need to come with me." A voice came from behind the light. "I can protect you. I can protect all of you."

"Bale? I mean, Uncle Dek? Is that you?" Josh asked.

"Yes! It's me! We have to go now!" Bale replied. "Turn off the lights!" Bale commanded the driver.

Josh ran up to Bale and hugged him as the lights turned off. "How did you get away? How is Dad?"

"It's not safe here on the streets. We have to get you out of here." Bale said.

"Where are we going?" Josh asked.

"We are going to get your dad?" Bale said.

"How?" Josh asked.

"Trust me," Bale said.

As Josh and the friends slowly began to walk towards Bale's van with their hands up, Barry jumped back in while it was still running. Yashi jumped into the passenger seat as Barry put the van into reverse, slammed on the gas pedal, and sped off.

"Let him go!" Bale told the other men who were with him. "They are not why we are here." He turned his attention to Josh, "You are why we are here."

In the confines of the van, a mix of relief and confusion lingered. The air was thick with tension as questions raced through everyone's minds. Brittany glanced at Josh, her eyes revealing concern and curiosity. Terra, Yashi, and Bub exchanged uncertain glances, unsure what to make of the sudden events.

As the van sped through the city streets, Josh turned to Bale, desperate for answers. "What's going on, Uncle Dek? Where's Dad?"

Bale hesitated for a moment before responding. "Your dad is safe, Josh, but we're not out of danger yet. We need to regroup and figure out our next move."

Josh, still seated next to Bale, couldn't shake off the feeling of uncertainty. "Uncle Dek, what happened back there? Why are they after us?"

Bale sighed, choosing his words carefully. "Josh, what you and your friends discovered about ProTech has put all of you in great danger. There are forces at play that want to keep the truth hidden. Your dad and I have been working to expose those seeking control and manipulation."

The gravity of the situation weighed heavily on Josh. "But why target us? What do they want?" Bale hesitated before responding. "You have a gift, Josh. The ability to do beyond what others think you can. It's a rare and powerful skill, and those who know about it will stop at nothing to harness that power for their own agenda."

Meanwhile, a tense journey unfolded in the other group led by Thomas. Each member moved cautiously, aware of the potential threats lurking in the shadows. The radio remained silent, signaling a commitment to stealth and secrecy. Ezzie, Abby, Ty, Deborah, and Caden moved silently through the darkness, their senses heightened by the looming danger.

Back in the van, Barry's energetic demeanor returned as he navigated the city's intricate layout. "This situation is like a real-life action movie! Breaking Stuff with Barry meets The Great Escape! And now I have Sushi Man with me, the great superhero!"

"Barry, why did you escape and not go with Bale?" Yashi asked.

Barry glanced at Yashi with a grin. "The license plates. I noticed that the license plate on the front of the vehicle chasing us and the one with

Josh's uncle was the same." His countenance changed, "Something is not right about this! I can feel it."
Yashi was shocked at Barry's observation skills, almost like he was riding with Sherlock Holmes.
"Hey, bro," Barry said, "Lighten up! Laughter is the best medicine, you know? Plus, we got the element of surprise on our side!"

As the van approached the city's outskirts, the city lights dimmed, and the urban chaos gave way to the calm of the rural surroundings. Barry took a deep breath and said, "We're getting closer to the bridge."
As the van approached the bridge, Thomas' group emerged from the shadow to flag down the van.
Looking into the van, Thomas sternly asked Barry, "Where's Josh? Where's everyone else?" Caden then moved angrily to Barry and grabbed him by the collar, "Where's my sister?" Abby and Ezzie comforted Deborah as she began to cry out in shock.
"Bro! His Uncle Dek took him! There was nothing we could do!" Barry said.
Ty moved between Caden and Barry. "I knew this was a bad idea." Thomas angrily said as he pointed towards Barry. "Now look where Adventures with Barry got us!"
"It's not his fault," Ty said as he stood before Thomas to redirect his attention away from Barry.
"Don't worry," Yashi said, "We know where they are going!"
"How?" Deborah asked.
"I have my tracer on Bub. He can't really go anywhere without me."
"How do we track it?" Abby asked.

"It's on my phone," Yashi said.

"We need to get to Martinsville and make a plan," Ty said.

Caden released his grip and said, "I'm sorry. I don't know what I would have done in that situation either."

Thomas stepped back and began to move towards the van. "I'm sorry, too. I just got upset." Thomas moved as well to get into the van.

Barry got into the driver's seat, "Are you ok with Aerosmith?"

"Not now, Barry!" Yashi replied.

The van crossed the bridge, leaving the city behind for now.

Chapter 26

Friends List

As the van continued on the streets, Terra looked outside and saw the city street named Spinner's Cove.
"Where are we going?" Terra asked.
"To see your dad," Bale replied.
As he said that, the city lights of Spinner's Cove were transitioned to darkness. Suddenly, there was a gravel road that the van turned off. They began to wind back through a deep forest for what seemed like miles. Slowly the path opened to a large field with a large concrete structure sitting in the back of the property that looked like the combination of a military compound and mansion. Josh had flashbacks to Bale's house, but there was something different as there was more darkness surrounding the compound. Almost as if secrecy was admired even though it was intimidating in its presence.
"Where are we?" Josh asked.
"This is Cokesbury Estate," Bale said.
"Cokesbury Estate? Is this our grandfather's place? What did you do, Bale?" Josh began to ask, holding back tears, realizing he had been deceived.

Brittany reached over and embraced Josh's hand to give him courage in the moment. Josh looked back and tried to hold in his emotions.

As they drove through the imposing walls, and guards stood as a fortress of power and influence. As they went through the gates, within its confines, Josh found himself at the epicenter of a grand design orchestrated by a man he had never met—his grandfather, Victor.

When they exited the van, Bale and the guards ushered Josh into the compound's central section. Josh looked back and saw his friends being directed by armed guards to a different section. Josh noticed something similar about the guards but couldn't place it immediately.

Josh entered onto an elevator that had light music playing in the background, almost uncharacteristic of the tone the compound presented. When the doors opened, Josh saw an old man seated on an intricately carved chair. He motioned for Josh to join him. Josh could feel how the room resonated with an air of authority that demanded obedience. And for the first time, he met his grandfather.

"Josh, my grandson," Victor spoke, his voice resonating with a subtle command. "Sit. We have much to discuss."

As Josh sat opposite his grandfather, he couldn't help but feel a sense of trepidation. Though filled with luxury, the room seemed to close in around him. Standing to the side, Bale wore an expression that betrayed a mixture of regret and resentment.

Victor fixed his penetrating gaze on Josh. "You are the heir to a legacy, Josh. A legacy that demands strength, power, and influence. It is time you embrace your destiny."

Grappling with the sudden revelation, Josh felt an invisible weight settle on his shoulders. "What legacy? I never knew you existed until now. Why did you keep yourself hidden from us?"

Victor, unmoved by sentimentality, replied, "I kept myself hidden to protect you. The world is not as simple as it seems, Josh. There are forces at play beyond your understanding. Forces that require a guiding hand, a hand that has been mine but now must be yours."

Bale, standing in the periphery, shifted uncomfortably. Victor's gaze, like a laser, found its mark. "Bale," Victor chided, "was entrusted with a task he failed to accomplish. He lacked the strength and vision necessary to achieve my goals."

Bale, a man haunted by the weight of expectation, bowed his head to acknowledge his failure. It was failure due to not standing up against his father. It was failure for not protecting Josh. Victor, however, shifted his attention back to Josh, dismissing Bale as inconsequential in the grand scheme.

"I trusted him," Victor replied.

"Where is my father? I want to see him now." Josh said sternly with an air of command.

"Don't worry about your dad, Josh. He's in good hands." Victor replied. "I have watched you, Josh," Victor continued. "You possess a strength of character, a resilience that can shape the destiny I have envisioned. With their misguided ideals, the Protectors stand in the way of progress. It is time for you to assert your authority and bring order to the chaos they have sown."

Josh, torn between familial loyalty and the expectations thrust upon him, sought clarity. "What do you want from me, Grandfather? Why am I the key to your plans?"

Victor, a master of manipulation, leaned forward, his eyes locking onto Josh's. "You are the key because you carry the blood of a lineage destined for greatness. How do you think this all came about? By accident. No! It was by taking every opportunity for power to be grasped and held. I offer you the chance to shape a new world where order and purpose reign supreme. A world where you reign supreme and do not have to live in the shadows."

"Do you mean like you live in the shadows?" Josh asserted. "I have found my family in the Protectors. They believe in a world where everyone can live in harmony. They believe in a world of truth. I can't turn my back on that."

Victor, undeterred by Josh's resistance, countered with persuasive rhetoric. "Harmony, my boy, is an illusion created by those who fear change. The world requires a firm hand, a hand that can mold it into a utopia of progress. The Protectors, blinded by their idealism, cannot bring true change." Victor stated, "Josh, don't be fooled. Your grandfather's vision is one of control, not freedom. The power he seeks comes at the cost of individuality and choice."

Suddenly from the corner of the room a voice rang out, "You don't have to do anything he says." It was Bale. "You can make the right choice, not the choice like I made. You are brave and strong. I am not."

"Silence!" Victor shouted. "Your time has come and gone." He pressed a button on his desk.

The door flew open and two men came in and moved towards Bale. Josh sensed how Bale was forced to act to bring him there and he could sense how Bale was trying to change his mind. The men grabbed Bale by the arms and began to drag him out of the room. "I may even be done with you if it wasn't for your sister," Victor said as they were taking Bale out of the room.

Josh was shocked at what he just witnessed. He turned his focus back to Bale, "Mom, what do you want from my mother?" Josh asked.

"Nothing!" Victor tried to downplay the anger he had just expressed. "I just want her here to see what could have been hers. But for you, Josh, this could all really be yours."

Victor stood and began to walk around the chair where Josh was seated.

He put his hand on his shoulder, "Imagine for yourself a world where what Josh says goes!" Imagine a place where you can be with your friends and family as much as you desire. Imagine having all the power to get whatever you want. Imagine having Noah back again." Suddenly, a concealed doorway slid open in a corner of the room, revealing a figure obscured by shadows. A sleek, human-like form emerged. Josh had the adjust his eyes. "This, Josh, I believe is your companion, Noah." Victor declared. "A manifestation of technological prowess, a symbol of the future you can shape. Noah is yours to command, a testament to the power that awaits you."

"Noah, is it really you?" Josh asked in amazement. He stood and put his two fingers up. Noah stared at Josh's fingers and reached up his fingers, similar to Josh's. In that moment, Josh could sense that something was different. While the AL-LI looked like Noah, he could sense there was something different in his reaction and expression.

Victor, perceiving Josh's internal struggle, sought to exploit the vulnerability. "You must choose, Josh. The Protectors or a destiny that transcends their limited vision. Embrace your legacy, and together, we shall shape a future that benefits our future generations."

Josh realized that he needed to find a way to leave the room and begin to find a way to escape. "I need time," Josh said.

"Fine, I will give you to the morning," Victor said. "After that, you will either be with me or removed."

"Removed?" Josh said. "What does that mean?"

"Do you really want to find out?" Victor asked.

Victor hit a button and two guards came in and began to be escorted out of the room.

"Can Noah come with me?" Josh asked.

"I think it is better that he stay with me for now." Victor replied. "Take him to the Watch Room."

As the doors shut behind him, the guards commanded, "Come on let's go!" As they turned a corner, suddenly, a guard came up from Josh with his face somewhat obstructed and said, "I can take him from here. You guys go on break."

Looking at each other and excited about the offer of an early break, one of them replied, "Ok thanks, the Watch Room is where he goes."

Then the other guard said, "And make sure you lock it."

"Got it." The new guard replied.

Once they arrived to the door, the guard grabbed him and pulled him into a corner of the hallway.

The guard took off his hat. It was Ryan.

"Are you ok, Josh?" Ryan said as he looked him over and turned his head from side to side to make sure no one was coming.

"How did you get away?" Josh asked with total surprise at Ryan's presence.

"Well, there are things you need to know and things I haven't told you about me," Ryan said. "Let's just say that I have a knack for getting in and out of places. We've got to get you out of here."

"What about my friends and my dad?" Josh asked. "He has kidnapped Bub, Terra, and Brittany."

"Oh, I didn't know they were here, especially Bub," Ryan replied. "I only heard about your arrival."

"How is my dad?" Josh asked.

"He's fine. He's tired." Ryan replied.

"Can I see him?" Josh asked.

"I don't think that would be a good idea because of all the guards." Ryan. "But I can give him a message."

"Please tell him help is on the way and that I love him," Josh said.

"Will do!" Ryan said. "For now, you have to play along with everything. But let me find a way to get everyone out."

"I am sure there is a plan coming from the Protectors of how to help. Barry and Yashi got away and they know how to find the other Protectors to tell them what's happening." Josh said.

"Ok, I can help them find a way to get in and for you guys to escape" Ryan said. "I need a radio." He muttered to himself as he closed the door.

Chapter 27

Mother Board

The night hung heavy over at Desirae and Bradley's house, as Barry, Yashi, Caden, Deborah, Ezzie, Abby, Ty, and Thomas were gathered around the kitchen table with a single radio sitting on the table humming the white noise of the airwaves, with the anticipation of any kind of message to come through. The shock of the how the events had transpired were still resonating in everyone's minds.
"We have to do something." Thomas broke the silence.
"They are expecting us though. It's almost like a trap." Abby said.
"I'm sure they are, but there has to be something that we can do." Ty said.
The hum of everyone talking began to increase as ideas were being shared across the table.
Slowly and unknowingly at first, the white noise began to break up and a voice began to come through.
"Everyone be quiet." Ezzie shouted out.
"Protectors…Protectors…" were the sounds coming through the radio.
"Who is that?" Ty asked.

"Protectors...Protectors...this is the truck man."
"The truck man?" Thomas asked. "Is this a trick by Belliston?"
"Come in...Protectors...this is the truck man." Broke through the soundwaves again.
"Ryan!" Yashi yelled out like he had won a prize. "It's Ryan, I promise you."
"It's a trap!" Abby said. "Did he get caught?"
"Do we trust Ryan?" Ty asked.
Deborah grabbed the radio and clicked the talk button twice. This was a common way that the Protectors would say yes to one another on the radios.
"Everyone is ok!" Ryan said, "But you need to hurry! Something happening soon!"
Deborah then picked up the radio to speak. As she rose the microphone to her mouth, Thomas grasped her hand and said, "Remember they can still track us."
"Truck man come in." Deborah said.
"Tell them, Mom is coming. Tell them, the Protectors are coming."
"Yes mam!" Ryan responded immediately and with a sound of excitement.
"Meet me in the trees before Cokesbury Lane."
Deborah gave the receiver two clicks of the button and then turned it off.
"It's time to go!" Deborah said resolutely.
"And do what?" Ezzie asked.
"Get my family back!" Deborah replied. "I have an idea."

Room was scarce as everyone was riding in Barry's van to Cokesbury Lane. Deborah ordered Caden to stay at Desirae's and Bradley's house to be a last resort for help if something was to happen. Thomas, seated in the passenger seat, guided Barry with directions as they passed Spinners Cove.

As they approached Cokesbury Lane, they saw the flicker of light from the side of the road.

"That must be Ryan." Deborah said. "Pull over to the side."

The van stopped on the side of the road. Ty slid open the door as everyone peered into the darkness of the woods.

"I don't see him." Abby whispered to Ezzie.

"Me either." Yashi said as if he was listening in on their conversation.

Suddenly, Ryan slid to the open door from behind the van. It caught everyone by surprise to where there was a small gasp let out. He had obviously been running and was trying to catch his breath as he was bent over.

"Are you ok?" Ty asked.

Ryan held up his hand for a moment to hold the progress of the conversation.

"I got your message Deborah. We are set. But we have to act quickly. I don't know how long it will take for them to realize one of their trucks are gone." Ryan said.

To everyone's surprise they were unaware of the conversation that Deborah and Ryan had.

"So, what's the plan Deborah?" Thomas asked.

The truck approached the gates. Ryan was driving and pulled up to the main gate and rolled down his window. In the passenger seat was Ty wearing a similar outfit as Ryan.

"What do you have?" the guard asked.

"We have some of the Protectors. They are in the back. Found them one the way to Martinsville." Ryan said trying to match the tone of the guard.

"That's where they thought they would be!" the guard said with an air of comradery. "Take them to the rooms. I'll let Japheth know."

"Ok! Will do!" Ryan said as he pat his hand against the side of the truck door as a signal to everyone that they were in.

As the gate lifted up, everyone in the back was able to grasp the vastness of the compound. Thomas and Barry were dressed up also as guards.

When they stopped the truck, Ryan and Ty quickly got out and had Thomas and Barry to pull out Abby and Yashi. "We have to move quickly." Ryan whispered. "In about 10 seconds, there will be guards swarming this area."

As they all got out, Ryan walked over to a set of doors and scanned a card that let them in.

When they walked in, they were greeted by two guards standing there with their electric shock guns. "Hey, you aren't supposed to be here!" one of them said.

"Wait! I have the orders right here to bring them to the rooms." Ryan said as he casually walked between them to get them to turn their attention to them and not to everyone behind them.

"See!" Ryan held up a paper and then suddenly Thomas and Ty grabbed them from behind and they dropped their shock guns.

Abby and Barry immediately picked up the shock guns and held it to their faces.

The guards held up their hands in surrender.

"Come in here." Ryan pulled everyone into a room next to where they were.

They removed their radios. Then they took off one of their boots and a sock and put it in their mouth. Then they took their belts and put it around their mouths to hold it in place. Thomas had some zip ties and was able to tie their hands behind their backs and their ankles so they couldn't move.

They then took Abby and Yashi and put zip ties around their wrists but it was loose just to keep the perception of being tied up as they walked around.

"We have to make it to the server room first." Ryan said. "It is just before the rooms where everyone is being held. Then we have to wait for the signal from Deborah."

"Ok let's go, but make sure that we walk together." Thomas said.

As the group left the room, they tried to walk with military precision, ever cautious of the need to get to the server room as soon as possible. When they came to a hallway, Ryan held up his hand to pause the progress of the group. "Wait here and let me check." He scanned a card and slipped into a dark room that had a buzz.

While they were waiting, Barry began to act as if he was working on some of his karate moves. "Can you please wait to do that?" Thomas said.

"Man, I'm just getting warmed up." Barry replied.
"Well, if someone sees you, they are going to question us." Thomas replied.
"No bro! They are going to think, I don't want to mess with him." Barry said as he chopped in the air again.
Everyone rolled their eyes.
Ryan's face suddenly emerged from the closed door. "Ok the coast is clear, hurry!"
The group shuffled into the room and shut the door behind them.
"We are in the server room. Deborah you are go!" Ryan said over a radio. "Ty be the lookout on the door. Ezzie you are a go!"
In the back of the truck, Ezzie sat with a laptop opened. She replied on the radio, "Ok thanks Ryan!"
She typed away furiously and with great intention.
She then spoke on the radio. "Deborah, we are ready."
The voice over the radio said, "Go!"
Suddenly, all the outside lights of the compound turned off. The guards all began to wonder what was happening.
Then with a few taps on her keyboard, Ezzie was able to hit a button and control the spotlights of the compound. She directed them all to the center of the courtyard where a lone Deborah was standing.

Clad in a simple yet resolute demeanor, Deborah presented herself as a singular force challenging the stronghold of darkness.
"I want to see my father!" Deborah shouted.
Her presence drew the immediate attention of the guards. They all began to shout at her for her to freeze and hold her hands up.

Deborah, resolute in her mind, said again and louder, "I want to see my father! Victor the game is over!"

The guards all scrambling on the radios began asking for commands from their superiors.

With a few more key strokes from Ezzie, all the screens in the compound were displaying Deborah standing on the courtyard.

Victor looked up from his regal chair and realized how Deborah was standing without his knowledge.

He ran over to his desk and pushed a button. "Bring all the Protectors to me. Now!"

He then pressed another button and began to speak over an intercom system that could be heard over the entire courtyard.

"Deborah," Victor spoke, his voice carrying the weight of authority. "To what do I owe the pleasure of this unexpected visit?"

Undeterred by the grandeur surrounding her, Deborah fixed her gaze upon the room where Victor was watching. "I've come for my son, my husband, my brother and my friends. I know what you've done, the lies you've woven, and the darkness you've embraced. I won't let you destroy him."

A sardonic smile played upon Victor's lips as he looked down on her. "Ah, the maternal instinct—a force that blinds one to the greater truths. Josh is where he belongs, among those who understand the true nature of power."

Deborah's resolve intensified, fueled by a conviction anchored in faith. "Your version of power is a perversion of God's design. I won't stand idly by while you manipulate and control. Release Josh and the others.

Your reign ends tonight." She said with ever more intensity as her words echoed through the grand compound.

"Bring her to me!" was the sole command that resonated across the courtyard.

Suddenly, she was met by a gathering of guards that began to escort her towards the main building.

Suddenly in the closet, Ryan heard a commotion. It was Japheth and Aiden in the hallway. He cracked open the door to hear them.

Aiden commanded Japheth. "Bring them all to Victor, even Josh."

"Yes sir." Japheth replied.

Ryan closed the door slowly.

"They are all getting moved. We need to get back to Ezzie at the truck and be ready to go." Ty said.

"Yes, let's go!" Thomas said.

The group opened the door and began to move down the hallways again. The guards were rushing around at the commands coming in to secure the compound.

They were all able to get back to the truck.

"We have to follow Deborah's orders and get out." Abby said.

"Right." Thomas replied.

"What can we do?" Ty asked.

"Let's go to the police. We know they are kidnapped. Even if it means we are caught." Ezzie said.

"That's right." Thomas said.

As they were sitting in the back of the truck, Barry and Yashi saw how Bub, Terra, and Brittany were being escorted by the guards to the main room.

"Come on Sushi dude." Barry whispered to Yashi.

Barry and Yashi slipped out of the back of the truck and began to follow the guards carrying the others.

After Ryan drove the truck out of the facility, they realized that Barry and Yashi were not in the back.

"Now we can say that they have kidnapped the kids." Thomas said.

"The police will have to respond."

"That's right, lets hurry." Abby said.

As Deborah entered the room she was met by the cold and calculating Victor sitting in his chair.

"My daughter!" Victor said with tone of sadistic sarcasm. "Always the innovator. Always the one that could figure it out. And now look at you. A woman of faith."

He paused for a moment and stood up.

"Your faith blinds you, Deborah. You fail to see the inevitability of change," Victor asserted, his eyes ablaze with a deceptive zeal. "I wanted to offer you power, prosperity, and a legacy that transcends the limitations of mortal existence. Embrace the truth, and your son may find favor among the chosen."

Deborah, resolute in her conviction, countered with a fervent plea. "The only truth worth embracing is the light of God's love. You've twisted that truth to suit your ambitions. Release Josh, Cal, and my brother and let the Protectors go free. Valley Hills deserves a future free from the shadow you cast."

Victor, his facade of superiority momentarily shaken, recoiled at the invocation. "And just how do you think you will give Valley Hills a future? I am the future! Josh is the future!"

"There is no future with you!" Deborah sharply replied.

"We will see about that." Victor said.

There was a knock at the door. Japheth entered with Josh and Bale and pushed them down into chairs across from Victors desk.

"Good Japheth! Tell Aiden to come here!" Victor said.

"Aiden, is he your new legacy?" Deborah asked as she looked at Josh to reassure him.

"Let's just say that Aiden gets it." Victor said. "For Aiden, he doesn't make emotional bonds. He simply does what I ask. Not like many of you. But all we need now is for Josh to make the right choice."

"Josh?" Deborah asked.

"Yes Josh!" Victor replied.

"If he wants to have it all, he can have it all. He can carry on the family legacy. He can have the power. He can have the control." Victor said.

Josh felt the weight of an impending choice—one that would shape the trajectory of his destiny and the fates of those entwined in the tapestry of Valley Hills.

Victor, the patriarch of a legacy built upon power and control, regarded Josh with a calculating gaze. His eyes, windows to a soul hardened by the pursuit of dominion, conveyed a resolve that brooked no opposition. Beside him, Bale, the loyal yet conflicted uncle, stood as a testament to the familial complexities entwined in the family.

Deborah, Josh's mother and a beacon of maternal love faced Josh with unwavering determination. Her gaze, fixed upon Josh, emanated a spiritual strength that transcended the temporal challenges surrounding them. In this cosmic battlefield, where ideologies clashed, and destinies hung in the balance, Josh's heart bore the burden of a choice that extended beyond mortal comprehension.

"So, what's your decision Josh?" Victor asked.

As the silence stretched, a portal to the spiritual realm cracked open, inviting the unseen forces to witness the choices made within the crucible of human free will.

"Wait, before you give that decision, I have some friends here to help you." Victor replied.

Amidst the charged atmosphere, the friends—Bub, Terra, Yashi, and Brittany—and Josh's father, Cal, were ushered into the room by the guards followed by Noah.

As the Protectors joined the tableau of familial confrontations, Noah, the humanlike AI robot, stood at attention, a silent observer of the unfolding drama. In the quivering air laden with the weight of choices yet to be made, Noah's artificial consciousness processed the intricacies of human emotions—a fusion of logic and empathy that defied the limitations of his artificial existence.

Victor addressed Josh with a voice that resonated with a deceptive warmth. "Josh, my grandson, the time has come for you to embrace your true destiny. Your friends, these Protectors, are a fleeting presence in the grand tapestry of power that awaits you. Choose wisely, and you shall inherit the legacy that befits your family. And so, to help you make the decision, here is what I am offering. If you say no, you will be removed."

"Removed?" Josh asked.

"Well, let's just say your memory will be removed." Victor said as he unveiled a syringe on the table. "In this syringe, I have the ability to remove your memory from ever knowing that you were a Protector. Really from knowing anyone or anything." He held up the syringe in his hand. "But if you say 'Yes.' I will let your friends and family go! I will even let them continue to live in Valley Hills freely."

"Don't do it, Josh! He's bluffing" Deborah said.

Victor stood in front of Josh face to face, "You are the heir to a lineage that spans generations. Do not let the transient bonds of friendship cloud your judgment. The Protectors are a hindrance to the true path that awaits you."

Undeterred by the persuasive rhetoric, Deborah stepped forward, her eyes locked with Josh's. "Josh, remember who you are—the son of a loving God who values compassion, justice, and mercy. The path Victor offers is one of darkness and manipulation. Your true strength lies in the purity of your heart."

As the familial forces clashed in verbal warfare, the friends stood united, their unwavering gaze fixed upon Josh. Terra, a pillar of strength and resilience, spoke with a conviction that echoed through the room. "Josh, we've faced trials together, and our bonds run deeper than the blood ties that seek to manipulate you. Choose the path of love, and you'll find a strength that transcends the temporal."

Bub, reflecting a quiet determination, added, "We believe in you, Josh. Choose love, freedom, and the path that resonates with the goodness within your soul."

Brittany's eyes, conveying a mixture of vulnerability and steadfastness, whispered, "You're not alone in this, Josh. We stand together through thick and thin."

The room, suspended in the delicate balance between familial legacy and the bonds of friendship, awaited Josh's response. Amid this cosmic crossroads, Noah, the AI observer, remained poised to execute the commands that would alter the course of Valley Hills' narrative.

"What if I don't want this life?" Josh replied.

"Fine, let me help you some more." Victor said. "Noah, remove them."

Noah, revealed in his hand more syringes. He began to walk towards the friends to erase their memories. This irreversible act would sever the threads of connection that defined the relationships in Josh's life.

A solemn hush enveloped the room as Noah extended his artificial hand toward Terra, Bub, and Brittany. The seconds stretched into eternity, and Josh, standing at the nexus of destiny, felt the weight of a choice that transcended the boundaries of mortal understanding.

In that pivotal moment, as Noah prepared to execute the irreversible act, Josh's hand trembled with a surge of internal conflict. The room, echoing with the silent prayers of those who dared to believe in the transformative power of love, bore witness to a pause. This inexplicable hesitation defied the programmed precision of artificial intelligence.

Josh, his voice breaking through the silence, looked at Noah and held up two fingers and uttered a phrase that resonated with the depths of his soul. "Two of everything."

Noah, frozen during his programmed task, processed the unexpected command. The room, suspended in a state of collective anticipation, awaited the implications of Josh's cryptic declaration.

Victor held bewilderment while the friends, their eyes reflecting a mixture of confusion and hope, sought to unravel the situation.

"What does he mean—'Two of everything'?" Victor demanded, his tone betraying a flicker of uncertainty.

Josh, his gaze unwavering, addressed the room with a clarity that cut through the lingering tension. "I choose not to erase the memories that define me—the memories of family and friends. Instead, I choose a path that transcends. Love and familial bonds are not mutually exclusive. I will embrace both, for they are integral to the essence of who I am. I am a Protector!"

In the aftermath of Josh's resolute choice and the profound revelation within the heart of the compound, the air crackled with a tension that lingered like a fading storm. Victor's authoritative facade, momentarily shaken by Josh's choice, struggled to control the unraveling situation. Suddenly, in an act of rage and desperation, Victor looked at Noah and said, "Remove them all, beginning with him." As he pointed to Josh. This decree hung in the air like a spectral specter, threatening to extinguish the glimmers of hope that had begun to flicker within the room.

As Noah moved towards Josh, he caught the eye of Noah again. He looked him in his eyes and said, "My friend, two of everything."

Noah's eyes flashed. Josh noticed how something happened and his countenance seemed to change. Noah sharpened his focus and then his gaze widened to who Josh was, and suddenly he gave him a wink and held up his fingers.

Immediately, Victor stepped forward and tried to grab the needle from Noah's hand. At the same time, Bale reached for it at the same time. As they struggled to control the direction of the syringe, Bale began to say, "Father, there must be another way. Josh's choice has shown us that love and family need not be sacrificed. Let us find a path that does not involve the erasure of memories."

Victor, momentarily caught off guard by Bale's unexpected defiance, tried to pull away from Bale. However, Bale ballooned towards Victor to hold onto his hand to prevent him from moving it closer to Josh. Noah then leapt towards Victor which caused both Victor and Bale to fall to the ground.

Noah, then stood and picked up Victor and in one motion threw him across the room almost like he was a toy in an adult's hand and he landed on a couch that rolled backwards. Shocked by what was unfolding, Josh knew that Noah had gone into protection mode. Noah then progressed towards where Victor was lying on the ground slightly concussed by the impact of being thrown.

Josh ran and stopped Noah for a moment. "I must protect Josh." Noah said in what sounded like blind rage.

"Noah, stop!" Josh yelled and put his hand on Noah's arms to stop his progress. Noah continued to lean forward towards continuing his goal of reaching Victor.

"I must protect Josh." Rang again from Noah's mouth as he began to show his strength beyond what Josh could stop. Noah reached Victor and picked him up by the neck with one hand. Victor began to grasp Noah's arm as his breath was leaving him. "Help...help" were the squeaks that came from Victor's last few breaths that he could muster. Suddenly, there was a flash of sparks from the back of Noah's neck and the light of his eyes left. Noah's arm remain extended, but his grip relented as Victor fell to the ground, grasping for air.

Everyone looked as Josh held in his hand the programming board for Noah that came from the back of his head. It was the hardest thing for Josh to do, but he knew he had to let go of Noah.

The room, now draped in a solemn silence, witnessed the gradual deactivation of Noah's form. His eyes moist with grief and gratitude, Josh whispered, "You were more than a machine, Noah. You were a friend."

While grappling with the consequences of his actions, Victor approached Josh with an expression that mirrored a complex amalgamation of remorse and realization. "I... I did not anticipate the depth of your convictions, Josh. Perhaps I have been blinded by my pursuit of power. I am... sorry."

The moment was soon changed as a gasp of "Help" came from where Bale was lying on the ground. Deborah rushed over to Bale to find that the needle had been inserted into Bale's neck during the struggle and his body laid still not knowing what would happen next. Deborah was able to look at the needle and see that it had not been fully injected. She reached down and was able to pull the needle out and looked at her brother and said, "D, I got this!" She then proceeded to stand up and help Bale to his feet.

As they turned around, they were greeted with Victor standing before them. In a moment of trepidation, unsure of what his next action would be, they stood frozen. Suddenly, he launched towards them in a full embrace. Never before had he held his children in this way. He then proceeded to turn towards Josh and Cal and invite them into the family hug. As the tears came down their faces, they soon invited Bub, Terra, and Brittany to join them.

Victor then said, "You have shown me the error of my ways, Josh. I am willing to find a path toward unity that does not involve the erasure of memories."

Standing alongside his father, Bale added, "We can build a future that embraces the right foundation for our family. I didn't believe they existed at one time, but now I know they do. The threads of redemption are woven in our choices moving forward."

As the room breathed a collective sigh of relief, Josh, retreated from the group for a moment and stood beside Noah. He knew that while no one could ever replace the true Noah, he knew that there was not a need for Noah in his world anymore. He grabbed his arm that was extended and positioned it with the two fingers up to Noah's and in a final statement said, "Two of everything."

The room exploded in a moment when Aiden Belliston and numerous guards rushed into the room. "I want them all removed." He screamed. "Even Victor."

As the guard began to move towards everyone, everyone began to retreat except for Victor. He spread his arms in almost an act of protection between Aiden and the rest of the Protectors.

"Aiden, I was wrong. These are good people. I let control ruin my life until now."

"Stop!" Aiden said commandingly to the guards. "You think that all of this was about you? I knew that Bale couldn't handle it. I knew that little Joshy wouldn't be able to do it. So, I had to take things into my own hands. I am now in control. ProTech is mine completely."

"Aiden, it doesn't have to be this way. There's more to life than just power and Protech."

"Well, I don't think so!" Aiden pulled out his knife and began to lunge towards Victor.

His progress towards Victor was stopped as Josh launched between Aiden and Victor. Aiden stepped back with a face that showed the horror of the reality of what just happened.

The blade was driven into Josh's upper chest and was left in place. Josh in shock of the sight of the knife handle sticking out from his chest, unsure of what to do next, he fell back into the arms of Victor as the screams filled the room from everyone that had just witnessed the act.

Victor pointed to the door and yelled out as loud as possible, "Remove him."

He looked down and his hand was grasped by one of the guards.

"Let me go!" Aiden commanded. The grasp of the guard got stronger.

"I said, let me go." Aiden commanded again.

Victor screamed, "Remove him now. Call the police chief."

The guards attention suddenly turned towards Aiden. They rushed towards him and in a swift moment they picked him up and began to remove him from the room.

"Victor, I won't forget this!" Aiden screamed as his voice rescinded from the room as his feet flailed in the air. "I won't forget this!"

Victor began to comfort Josh in the pain, "You will be ok. You will be ok. I'm so sorry I let this happen to you. It's all my fault. I'm so sorry for everything. Josh"

Deborah and Cal came over and began to stroke Josh's face and tried to speak through the tears and groans of what they were witnessing.

Bub, Terra, and Brittany all began to huddle together as they were crying.

Victor jumped up and hit a button on his desk, "Prepare the helicopter. Now!"

Cal bent down and said, "My brave boy! Be strong a little longer."

He then scooped him up in his arms and said, "Let's go!" with a resolve unseen before.

In a moment, everyone rushed out of the room.

The doors burst open to the helipad with Victor running towards the helicopter. Yashi and Barry were standing nearby unaware of what happened to try and stop him at first. Their focus changed when Deborah ran out the door next and held it open for Cal carrying someone in his arms followed closely by Bale. As they looked closer, they realized it was Josh and he looked lifeless as the door to the helicopter slid open and everyone got in.

Yashi and Barry stopped their movement in shock. The door was soon opened again as Bub, Terra, and Brittany all followed with faces of remorse and terror at what they were seeing of their friend. As the helicopter lifted off the ground, the realization that this could have been the last time of seeing their friend rushed over the group.

"What do we do?" Terra asked as her emotions revealed a transparency never experienced by the others.

"I don't think there's much we can do now." Yashi said.

"There's only one thing we can do." Brittany said. "Pray."

Bub, who had been standing apart from the others watching the helicopter fly away off in the distance, said softly, "I want to do it."

"What did you say bro?" Barry asked.

"I want to say the prayer." Bub turned around with a confidence exuding as never before. "He was my best friend and that's what we do for each other when we can't do anything else. We pray."

The group gathered around and closed their eyes in a moment of silence as Bub began to lead them in a time of prayer. When they had finished, they all got into Barry's van and started towards the hospital.

Conclusion

Restored

The beeps of the heart monitor echoed through the room. Josh slowly opened his eyes unaware of his surroundings. He began to hear in the room the conversation, "He's waking up. Get the doctor."

Josh opened his eyes again to the room filled with Deborah, Cal, Victor, and Bale.

How do you feel son? Cal asked.

Deborah reached forward and stroked his face again with tears running down her face, "You are so brave my son."

As Victor and Bale watched, soon the door opened with the presence of the doctor and his team of nurses.

"Please step back for a moment."

He held a small light up to Josh's eyes and flashed them across his face. Josh winced at the brightness of the light and asked, "What happened?"

"You have someone watching over you. The knife penetrated just above your heart and lungs to where there was no damage to those organs. Fortunately, you were brought here immediately."

"So, he will be okay?" Bale asked.

"Yes, he may not be able to use his right shoulder for a little bit and there will be some pain and a scar, and he should definitely get some rest. But he should recover quickly. I will want to follow up. But for now, rest!"

"Yes sir!" Josh replied as he slumped back in relaxation.

Josh had been awake when his mother walked into the room. There are some friends that are here to see you.

Soon the room was filled with Bub, Yashi, Terra, and Barry.

Barry hurried to Josh's bed and gave him a pat on the shoulder, without realizing it was the shoulder that was hurt. Josh's face showed the pain immediately with a little growl, "Barry!"

"Oh, sorry dude." Barry replied.

"No problem" Josh replied sarcastically.

"We are glad you are ok." Terra said. "I was beginning to worry about you."

"Yeah man, how else would we be able to make it without our fearless leader." Yashi said.

"Oh, I'm sure you would have voted me out early enough." Josh said with a small sound of laughter in his voice.

Bub then stepped forward with solemness, "Josh, seriously, we prayed for you and I'm grateful you are ok."

Josh realizing the seriousness of the moment nodded and replied, "Thanks bro!"

"I think there is someone else that wants to see you." Barry said.

As the group separated towards the door, Brittany stood there. She rushed to Josh's side and put both hands on his face and gave him a kiss.

"I think he is going to be ok." Barry said.

"Man, when can I get hurt in the hospital?" Bub asked sarcastically.

Brittany sat on the side of the bed and Josh cuddled her under his arm.

"Guys, thank you! We are Protectors and we stay together! I wouldn't be here today without each one of you!"

The friends stayed a little longer together telling the stories of everything that happened. Barry and Bub seemed to act out the most while everyone else sat back and laughed. For the first time in a long while, they had a moment of normalcy in the lives!

In the wake of the transformative events that unfolded within the confines of Valley Hills, the community stood at the threshold of a new era—a testament to the enduring power of love, forgiveness, and the pursuit of redemption. The tapestry of lives, intricately woven with threads of strife and resilience, now bore the marks of a shared journey. This journey transcended the boundaries of familial ties and ideological divisions.

The aftermath of Josh's resolute choice reverberated through Valley Hills, leaving behind a landscape marked by the echoes of a tumultuous past. The reunited family—Josh, Cal, Deborah, Victor, and Bale—walked together, their footsteps a testament to the potential for redemption that lay dormant within the human heart. The Protectors—Bub, Terra, Yashi, Brittany, and Barry—also formed a collective testament to the strength forged through trials.

As the community emerged from the shadow of the aftermath of the events of the compound, Valley Hills found itself at a crossroads. The scars of conflict remained, etched into the fabric of the town's history. Still, there existed an opportunity for healing—a chance to mend the tears that had threatened to unravel the very fabric of the community. The newfound unity within the Protectors marked a pivotal turning point. Humbled by the consequences of his relentless pursuit of power, Victor stood on the precipice of transformation. The once-authoritarian patriarch now recognized the fallacy of erasing memories as a means to an end. His acknowledgment of the error in his ways signaled a potential renaissance—a chance for the Valley Hills to rebuild.

Standing alongside his father, Bale embodied the resilience that accompanied the pursuit of redemption. His decision to defy Victor's commands in favor of a path grounded in compassion and understanding spoke volumes about the transformative power of love. The reunion of the family underscored the potential for redemption within even the most fractured relationships.

In the heart of Valley Hills, the community's collective consciousness grappled with the remnants of a tumultuous past. Once declared public enemies, the Protectors now found themselves navigating the terrain of acceptance. Thomas, the steadfast leader, carried with him the wisdom gained through the trials that had forged the bonds of their fellowship.

Bub, Terra, Yashi, Brittany, and Barry, each bearing the scars of their unique journeys, stood united in the face of an uncertain future. Their friendship, tested by the crucible of adversity, emerged as a beacon—a testament to the enduring strength within the bonds of shared hardship as they were soon joined by others stepping out of the shadows.

Josh, having witnessed the sacrifice of Noah and the unraveling of his grandfather's authoritarian vision, grappled with the weight of responsibility. The loss of Noah, left an indelible mark on Josh's heart. Yet, even in that loss, Josh found a renewed sense of purpose—a commitment to forging a path that embraced the complexities of familial ties and the broader tapestry of community.

As Valley Hills embraced the dawn of a new era, the community sought to reconcile with its past while charting a course toward a future defined by unity and understanding. The tapestry of redemption, woven with threads of sacrifice, forgiveness, and love, unfolded against the backdrop of a town determined to rise above the fractures that had threatened its very foundation.

Made in the USA
Monee, IL
01 January 2025